MISS MARY MARGARET

MISS MARY MARGARET

BOOK II

Mary Frances Hodges

iUniverse LLC
Bloomington

MISS MARY MARGARET
BOOK II

iUniverse books may be ordered through booksellers or by contacting:

iUniverse LLC
1663 Liberty Drive
Bloomington, IN 47403
www.iuniverse.com
1-800-Authors (1-800-288-4677)

ISBN: 978-1-4917-1406-5 (sc)
ISBN: 978-1-4917-1408-9 (hc)
ISBN: 978-1-4917-1407-2 (e)

Library of Congress Control Number: 2013920804

Printed in the United States of America.

iUniverse rev. date: 12/09/2013

CONTENTS

CHAPTER 1

WE MOVE TO LITTLE ROCK

I never dreamed I would move to Little Rock, Arkansas, just as I never dreamed I'd marry a Yankee. How quickly time passes, and you don't realize it. Every day is assumed to be just another day in an unending line. We never stop to realize how unique those days were until we look back, and wish we could recapture them. I followed my husband, Thomas Harwell, to Little Rock as he entered the politics of reconstructing Arkansas, which was devastated by the Civil War.

The last time I came to Little Rock, I was with my parents, neither of whom I have seen in several years. Neither my parents nor the town accepted my marriage to Thomas. Being a Union officer was more than they could tolerate initially, yet I loved Thomas. I have loved him each of the forty years, since we eloped to Fort Gibson, Indian Territory, during the last year of the war.

The boat trip down the Arkansas River was fascinating. I didn't want to sit in the ladies' parlor, so Tom and I stood on the deck so I could see the scenery. We were having an unusually warm spell for early December, so my fur lined cape with a hood kept me more than warm on deck. Tom had been down, and up, the river several times during the war, but this was only my second trip down the river. There was a poker game going on the boat, but Tom stayed with me. It was rare that Tom passed up a Poker game. He said it was to keep me from falling overboard. I hoped he just wanted to be with me; we were still very much in love.

We floated past thickly wooded areas, where sunlight could barely creep though the dense overlay of foliage; past the lush delta-looking land of McClean's bottoms; the small villages hugging the river bank for fear they might lose their sense of being. If the river should change its course, it would cut them off from the world, and the world's goods. That would lead to the villages' demise.

Sometimes we could see the men working near the river banks, struggling to build the railroad tracks that will not only cut the travel time up and down the river valley but also cause the end of steam boats plying the river.

People pass through our lives similarly, the way the landscape comes into view, as we float down the river and then glides away. So do our friends and acquaintances, who are with us for a little while, and then life experiences change, and the people in our lives change, and float away so to speak.

Time is just like the river. They both flow over rocky patches where one is not sure there is enough support to continue; plus, there are unseen dangers, represented by the snags partly sticking above the water. Then there are times of tranquility, but the flow never stops. Time gives us an ever changing view of human events. The variety of events impacts all of us individually, and, as a nation, which my husband fought so hard to save. I didn't realize that when we married, but now I realize how important it was to save the United States as a country.

It was easy to see when we were approaching Little Rock, as our beautiful capitol building came into view. Its white walls were gleaming in the sunlight, even though the view was of the back of the building. Our Capitol is beautiful on all sides.

When the boat docked at the Little Rock wharf, I was excited about the future and all the new experiences that were in store for both me and my husband. At that time I had, thankfully, no idea of the many moves across this entire country that lay ahead of us.

We checked into the Metropolitan Hotel, the most prominent hotel in town. Many of the Republican delegates to the Constitutional Convention were staying there. It was the unofficial Republican Party Headquarters. I met General Powell Clayton, who had also married a girl from Arkansas; John Sarber from Johnson County, who had only been a private, but had been the standing orderly for Colonel Cloud in the Second Kansas. John had become a lawyer, Thomas told me. John Garver, whose aunt and uncle lived next door to my parents' house in

Van Buren, was there. I met Thomas, for the first time, at a tea at the Garver's home.

The day Arkansas voted to leave the United States, I was in Little Rock with my parents. Papa was a delegate to the Secession Convention from Crawford County, Arkansas. All the delegates, except one, voted to leave the Union. The mood at dinner was jubilant that night. No Yankee could beat us!

The mood at dinner, the first night Thomas and I had were at the hotel in Little Rock, was enthusiastic, and optimistic, just as it had been four years earlier, but for a different reason. The delegates were hopeful that their work to write a new state constitution would create one that would be accepted by the U.S. Congress. Then Arkansas could rejoin the United States. It was obvious by the dinner conversation that not everyone held the same viewpoint on many issues. It should be an exciting convention!

Since the end of the war, Arkansas had been drifting in chaotic limbo. Some people refused to believe that the Confederacy was not victorious, and failed to see why things couldn't just go back to the way they were before. It ended up that the state was placed into a military district governed by Major E. O. D. Ord, whose office was in Holly Springs, Mississippi. But that had finally been resolved and elections were called for.

It was difficult to hold elections in Arkansas at that time, because in order to vote both the former Confederate soldiers and the former Union soldiers had to sign a loyalty oath that they would be true to the U. S. Government. Many of the ex-Confederates refused to sign, and the Confederate officers weren't allowed to vote, period. So it was hard to find enough qualified men to hold an election in some counties. Some counties didn't vote at all on whether or not to have the convention.

After dinner there were always brandy and cigars for the gentlemen, and the ladies would go into the parlor for demitasse coffee. Afterwards, Thomas and I would retire to our suite of rooms where he would give me, what he called, "a real good night kiss." He then would redress and return downstairs to play poker for several hours. He said it was that type of good night kiss that caused him to be so lucky at the Poker table. I was glad to accommodate him, but Tom already had the reputation as an expert poker player. Little did I realize then, that at some time in the future, Tom's poker winnings would be our only source of real income.

One Sunday, several weeks later, it was warmer than usual for that time of year, and Tom suggested we go for a walk. There hadn't been rain for several days and the walkways were dry. There were small patches of snow remaining, and I was so surprised that there were crocus in bloom sticking their heads up through the snow. Little Rock's being so much farther south than Van Buren, made Spring show early signs. When we reached the corner, we turned right and walked about half a block. We stopped before a cottage, and Tom asked me how I liked it. I thought it was charming.

"I bought it for you."

"You bought it?"

"Yes, I thought you would like it, but if you don't, I can sell it to someone else."

"Never, I love it! Look, there are rose vines growing all over the front fence, and vines growing up the trellises that frame the front porch!" Although they wouldn't be in bloom for several months, I looked forward to having roses just like at my parents' house.

"I have the key, would you like to go inside."

"Oh, Tom, yes. I can hardly wait. I can't believe you bought this for us!"

"Actually I bought it to please you."

"You most certainly pleased me!"

We went inside. It had a large front room, a smallish but adequate dining room, and two bedrooms. There was a small dressing room off one of the bed rooms. I was walking through the house so happy; I couldn't believe we were going to live here.

"Surely you didn't think we'd live at the hotel forever."

"Where ever we lived would be fine as long as you were there."

I hugged Tom and kissed him until I was out of breath.

Since it was the Sabbath, I wouldn't let Tom play poker that night, but I entertained him in his other favorite way. I was the one who felt lucky that night.

The next morning Tom handed me six, one hundred dollar bills, and told me he wanted me to fill the house with whatever furniture I liked. I just stared at the money.

"Sweetheart, if that isn't enough I can give you more."

"That's not the problem. I've never bought anything before."

"What do you mean?"

"I've never had to buy anything. Everything was provided for me."

It had never dawned on Tom that Mrs. Hughes, our housekeeper, had always done the grocery shopping, and before we left Van Buren, Tom surprised me by bringing home a whole variety of the latest fashion in dresses, which he had purchased on a trip to St. Louis. Every dress he brought me was also in the most fashionable colors. So many delightful colors to choose from! I didn't mind giving up the hooped shirts, but learning how to accommodate the bustle, when sitting, took some time for me to be comfortable with it.

There were dresses in mauve, lavender, magenta and a bright purple that my mother would never have approved of. All of the dresses came with decorative snoods. It was a whole new world of fashion. The only problem with the evening dresses was that they all had small trains, which presented a problem if Tom did not watch where he was stepping. Tom said he always wanted his wife to wear the latest fashion. He said I was too beautiful to wear anything drab. Many people commented on my beauty which really embarrassed me outwardly, but inside I was quite pleased. I didn't know how I was going to be accepted by the people in Little Rock, especially since I was a southern girl who had married a northern soldier.

"Maggie, go down the street to John Derry's furniture store and pick out whatever you want. John was a major with the 3rd Wisconsin, and a good man. I will stop by the store on my way to the Capitol, and tell him to expect you. If you spend more than that, I'll pay him the rest tonight."

"Wisconsin is a long way away. How did he get so far from home?"

"Same way I did" Tom said.

"Oh" I exclaimed "That was a dumb question."

"Major Derry fought in Arkansas, in fact, he lead an expedition to Fort Smith and crossed the river at Van Buren. He left twelve horses for us to shoe before his troops could head back to Little Rock. He liked Arkansas, just like so many of our soldiers did. It's warmer here, too. Wisconsin is really cold in the winter. John was so in awe of the abundance of foliage down here. He once said that he was sure that if he stood in the middle of a road very long, a vine would grow up his leg."

Tom thought Kansas was flat and ugly. He lived there before the war and had been active in politics there, as well.

I was excited, but felt intimidated about not understanding the value of money. John Derry had lovely furniture which he said belonged to a number of families who had abandoned their homes and just left the furniture behind. He tried to find relatives of the people so he could pay them for the furniture, but no one would tell him where the families went. He assumed the people were afraid harm would come to them, after the war, since they had been loyal to the Confederacy. Some apparently didn't want anyone to know where they had gone. He thought the people probably had gone to Texas or California.

I bought a settee and several occasional chairs with red velvet fabric framed by cherry wood, two small tables, and several table lamps, an ornate mirror, and lovely room rug with a pattern of large red and white roses against a sky blue back ground. I found a dining table with chairs that would seat six. I would have liked a larger table, but our dining room wouldn't accommodate it. There would barely be room for the side board. I also got a very large walnut armoire with cedar lining for the bedroom.

I fell in love with a beautiful antique bed. Mr. Derry said that a Mr. Horace Abercrombie bought it as a wedding present for his bride. The bed had been shipped up river from New Orleans to his plantation. His plantation was so large he even had a landing on the Mississippi River. Mr. Abercrombie was really too old to fight when the war broke out, but he insisted on joining the Confederacy. He fought in the Battle of Mark's Mills, and Mrs. Abercrombie, when she learned of his death, promptly died of a heart attack. They had only one daughter left by then. Their other six daughters died of illness, and a son was killed at the Battle of Jenkins Ferry.

Since the Abercrombie's no longer had slaves, and there were no able bodied men around to cut wood for them, the women had to use some of the furniture for fire wood in the winter. After her parents' deaths, their daughter sold all of the furniture that hadn't been burned. This bed was one of the few pieces that survived. Right after the war, the daughter moved in with an aunt in Little Rock. Mr. Derry bought the bed from the daughter, who told him the story of how they were ruined by the war. There was no matching dressing table, to go with the bed, but I found one in cherry to match the bed, and it went with it perfectly.

The bed was so beautiful; I would have given $600.00 for it alone. It was a combination of cherry and mahogany with a half tester. The underside of the tester was tufted beige velvet. I don't know if Thomas had to pay Mr. Derry any more money for my purchases or not. I didn't ask, and he never said. He did ask if I got everything I wanted. I thought my cup was running over, and then he said,

"How about some pictures, Maggie? Did you not see any you liked?"

I was so excited with all my purchases I had not even thought about pictures. I brought two pictures I had painted to Little Rock. Tom thought I was a really talented painter and suggested I just paint some pictures for the house.

I was pleased he was proud enough of my paintings that he wanted his friends to see them. The very next day I found a hardware store that sold paints and brushes, canvas and an easel. They weren't new but would be all right for the time being. The store did have a new piece of canvas I could use to cover a half-finished painting. I announced to Tom I was going to paint his portrait. He agreed, but said he wouldn't have time to sit still for very long periods at a time, until they got the new constitution matter settled. Then Tom said he could lie on the bed naked and I could paint his portrait while he slept. I told him that if I was going to paint a naked man it would have to be a younger one. Tom turned me over his lap and gave me a couple of love spanks.

The next day, Mr. Derry had two hired men deliver the furniture to the house and Mrs. Hughes helped me with where to place things.

Tom had surprised me by buying a hand-made Bensberg piano which was delivered the other furniture. I cried when I saw it. I had always heard how wonderful they were, but I had never seen or heard one before because they were made in Camden, Arkansas which was so far south in Arkansas there was no easy way to get one of them, in one piece, as far north as Van Buren.

I so loved to play the piano that had been a wedding present to my mother and was often asked to play for my parents' guests. They were always quite complimentary of my playing.

Mrs. Hughes came with us to Little Rock. Tom said it was self-preservation. I wasn't offended. Tom had joked, that I needed written directions to boil water, which was close to the truth. I was delighted she was here. Mrs. Hughes pointed out to me that we needed a mattress and new bed linens. I was embarrassed to learn that mattresses didn't automatically come as part of the bed. I had brought some linens from home, but she said a bed that lovely deserved new bed linens. Tom had realized I probably wouldn't think to buy linens, so he had given Mrs. Hughes some money to take me shopping.

Mrs. Hughes had been our housekeeper, and my salvation, in Van Buren. I had never learned any of the domestic arts. Aunt Marie and Uncle Henry, our slaves, did everything, but my mother took them with her when she fled to Washington, Arkansas. Plus, well-bred southern girls were not supposed to bother themselves with such things as cooking and cleaning.

Our cottage had a stable outback with two rooms over it. Mrs. Hughes, whose husband died at the Battle of Prairie Grove, stayed there. It already had some furniture in it. I supposed it was where the house slaves, of the previous owners, had stayed. Mrs. Hughes was pleased with the arrangement. Thomas paid her enough that she no longer had to entertain young gentlemen at night like she did in Van Buren, or so I thought.

That first night in the new bed was as exciting as the first night we came together as man and wife. It was our very own bed, in our very own house. Tom was obviously very excited too, and physically manifested it. I couldn't have been happier. After three years of marriage, our passion for each other was just as great.

Our house was only about a block away from Christ Episcopal Church. Since Tom left early to go to work, I would go to Morning Prayer practically every day. It was good to hear and say the familiar prayers. I had missed them so much. Reading from the Prayer Book everyday had helped keep me connected while in Van Buren.

Usually Tom and I slept late on Sunday mornings. During breakfast, Tom would take a pencil and circle all the lies *The Gazette* would tell about the convention and the delegates. The paper called it the "black and tan" convention because there were eight delegates who were black. I didn't understand what the tan was about, but I was sure it was not meant kindly. The paper even claimed that only one or two of the delegates could read or sign their name. That was simply not true. Eleven of the delegates were lawyers. Tom had even served in the Iowa State Legislature before the war.

Tom said that as soon as the Constitution was approved, John Price, the official Secretary of the Convention, was going to start a Republican newspaper so people could know the truth about what was going on.

At noon we would go out to eat with friends and would usually go to one of their homes for coffee and wine.

When we got home on Sunday evening, I would play the piano for several hours, and Tom usually fell asleep in a chair. Being President of the Convention was quite tiring.

CHAPTER 2

A FAMILIAR VOICE

One Sunday morning Tom had to go to an early meeting at the Capitol about seating some delegates from Ashley County, or some such. I didn't care about any of that. I took advantage of his leaving early to go to the regular church service. The priest celebrated the Eucharist, and it was the first time, in a long time, that I had been able to receive the body and blood of our Lord. As I was leaving church a women came up to me and introduced herself as Louisa Sadler. "I heard someone call you Mrs. Harwell. Is that right?"

"Yes it is, Mrs. Sadler." Mrs. Sadler was a slightly pump woman and a wisp of light brown hair had escaped from under her plain hat bedecked with small flowers that had seen better days, but what in the South hadn't seen better days?

She then asked the traditional southern question, asked of all strangers whom they meet: "Who are your people?"

I told her that my parents were Dr. Richard and Mary Jane Thompson of Van Buren. She asked my husband's full name, and when I told her Thomas Asbury Harwell. She got so excited. She started talking non-stop "I just moved here recently from Ringgold, Georgia, and there are so many Harwells in that area, the saying is that one could fire a gun in any direction and hit one of them." She rambled on, "The Harwells are all staunch Methodists, and a number of them were ministers. Is your husband from northern Georgia, too? I probably know his people. You tell your young man that John Wesley never left the Episcopal Church, and he should join you here."

I was trying to decide whether to lie to her about his being from Georgia, or tell the truth. That Tom was from Kansas would prompt questions I wasn't eager to answer. Plus the attitude of the church's members towards northerners was well known. Before I could say anything, a familiar man's voice said, "Mary Margaret." I turned around and there was my Poppa.

I threw my arms around his neck and started sobbing. He hugged me back and he took out a handkerchief to wipe my eyes. "Oh, Poppa! I didn't think I would ever see you again, nor that you would forgive me for eloping. Is Mother with you?"

"No, your mother isn't well. She took Swamp fever while in Washington. It flares up periodically. You couldn't buy a bottle of quinine in three states. I ran out of my health pills, so we had to wait unit we got back to Van Buren before I could make any more."

"Has she tried going to Pennywit Springs?"

"Yes, but the water in the springs hasn't done as much good as we had hoped. The area around the spring is a mess. The Federal troops tore the place up and even burned the mill and post office."

I just frowned and hung my head, and muttered that I was sorry. For all I knew Tom's 13th Kansas had done that.

"Your mother wanted to come, but just didn't have the strength, but she insisted I come so she could find out how many grandchildren we have."

"Oh Poppa, Thomas and I can't have children" I said with a lump in my throat. "I'm sorry"

"Maggie, there are doctors now who are specializing in women's problems. Have you seen one of them"?

"It's not me, Poppa. It's Tom. He'll have to explain it to you." I certainly could have explained it to him, that Tom was sterile, and why, but I wasn't comfortable talking about such things with my father especially on a public sidewalk. Such matters were rarely spoken of privately.

"But does he make you happy in your marriage?" I knew what he was actually asking. "Yes, Poppa, Thomas makes me very happy."

"Well, that's all that really counts."

"Aunt Marie and Uncle Henry are taking care of your mother this week." My father added.

"Oh, they came back with you?"

"Yes, I told them they were free and to go where ever they wanted to. They said they would stay with us because that was the only home they knew and they are really too old to be striking out anew at their age. I pay them a monthly wage, of course."

"What name did they take?"

"They said that they had always thought of themselves as Thompsons, and if we didn't care they would just keep that name. That was fine with me. Mother wasn't pleased, but you know how your mother is. Their son, Sam, took the name Freeman and headed west. They got word he is in California or Colorado, I am not sure which. The church Marie and Henry attend have special classes for their members to teach them to read and write. Marie plans to get good enough so she can write Sam a letter as soon as they know where to send it."

Mrs. Sadler was looking on bewildered. I had to introduce my father to her, or it would have been rude. I was happy to introduce him as Dr. Richard Thompson of Van Buren. Poppa said he was glad to meet her and then took my arm and turned me away toward the street. He said he had been standing there long enough to hear the conversation and realized I was in a fix.

"Was Thomas not able to come to church with you today?"

I swallowed hard. Tom never came to church with me, but I answered truthfully, "No, he had an emergency meeting at the State House; something about seating some delegates."

"Some things never change when it comes to legislation."

"Maggie, have you had breakfast?"

"No, I have always held to your teachings not to eat before taking the Eucharist." Poppa's folks were from England and very strict about the Anglican teachings.

"There a nice café on the other side of Maple Creek. There hasn't been much rain so we should be able to step across."

"What happened to the bridge such as it was?" My father asked. "I remember there being one."

"It was destroyed when the 3rd Minnesota captured Little Rock."

"There are so many new businesses. I'm glad Little Rock is coming back to life" he said. "Van Buren is recuperating too. There was so much damage." Unfortunately I already knew that, and that General Blunt ordered the Union soldiers to burn all the public buildings.

We entered the Friendship Café. A number of the parishioners from Christ Church were already there. Reverend Simpson soon joined the group, and I was delighted to introduce my father, a true Confederate, to him.

Poppa and I both enjoyed a typical southern breakfast: biscuits dripping with butter and honey, eggs, bacon and ham. The waitress offered us some grits, but we both declined. The people in southern Arkansas like grits, but Van Buren was far enough north in the state that the grits culture had not been a part of our lives. I thought they looked disgusting anyway.

After breakfast, I took Poppa to see our house. I was so proud of it. He seemed somewhat impressed, and especially with the fact I had picked out the furniture by myself. He commented that he has seen a similar rug with the big red and white roses on it, in a house in Natchez, and he wished he had bought such a rug for the Van Buren house.

"I wish you could stay with us, but we have only one bed. Tom is going to turn the other bedroom into an office."

"I've already checked into the Anthony House. I would be delighted if you and Thomas would dine with me tonight at eight."

"I am sure Thomas will be delighted to meet you. I have told him what a wonderful man and father you are."

We sat down in the parlor and Poppa said, "Well, Maggie, I probably shouldn't have gone off down to Washington, Arkansas and left you and your mother in Van Buren. I just thought it was the best thing for the Confederacy. I felt Aunt Marie and Uncle Henry could take good care of you. I mistakenly thought the Yankees wouldn't bother with Van Buren. I thought Ft. Smith would be their only interest, with the fort being there. I was wrong. I should have realized that Van Buren was the trade center for the area, so, of course, they were interested in capturing it."

"I've been told General Blunt burned five boats loaded with corn and cotton there at the wharf in Van Buren. Is that true?"

"Five boats were set on fire, but no one seems to know for sure if Blunt lit the torch, or if Confederates did."

"Aunt Marie and Uncle Henry did take good care of us, and you were right to leave a shot gun, even if it was against the law. Uncle Henry hunted when he could, but always had to be careful about going out. Between the Yankee foraging parties, and Confederates wanting to kidnap him. He had several close calls. Aunt Marie stretched the food as far as she possibly could. Things didn't get really bad until the war was almost over. After Thomas met me, he saw to it that we had enough to eat."

"Child, did you marry Thomas so you would have enough to eat?

'Oh, no Poppa, I truly love Tom"

"I want to thank him in person for seeing that you and your mother had enough to eat. I owe him a debt of gratitude"

"Thomas is a wonderful man, and I love him very much. I want you and mother to love him too. I think Mother actually liked him, it was the fact that he was a Yankee that she objected to. Did she tell you that he was a lawyer and in practice with Jesse Turner before we moved down here?"

"I had heard that and asked Jesse about it. He said that Thomas was a very good lawyer, and obviously devoted to you."

Poppa didn't ask about Thomas' divorce, and I was thankful I didn't have to discuss it with him. It was not my place to tell him about Eleanor, and how it wasn't a real marriage. That would be Tom's task if he asked. Poppa mentioned that our marriage could still be blessed by an Episcopal priest. I promised I would mention it to Thomas. I believe Thomas would agree to it if for no other reason than to keep me happy. I would really like to have the church's blessing.

"Poppa, Thomas is President of the Convention, I am quite proud of him"

"A wife should always be proud of her husband. I just wish we hadn't been forced to write another new constitution. The Constitution I helped write was a good piece of work, we just didn't give colored men the right to vote, so Congress turned it down. But enough of that talk."

Poppa went into the bedroom again and asked "Is that a Prudence Mallard bed?"

"I really don't know. Mr. Derry said something about its being a Mallard bed, but I didn't ask what he meant. I felt so dumb to start with."

"Mr. Mallard is considered the finest carver in the South. Your mother is going to be impressed."

That would be a first, I thought, but didn't say anything.

Poppa kissed me on the cheek, and said how glad he was to see me so happy. We hugged, and I promised him we would see him that night at dinner.

CHAPTER 3

MY FATHER MEETS THOMAS

As promised, we met Poppa that night for dinner at the Anthony House. That was the first time I had ever seen Thomas nervous. He shouldn't have been. He looked so handsome in his long cut-a-way frock coat and vest. The high white collar of his shirt was set off by the wide silk tie I help him make into a bow. I chose my mauve-colored evening dress as I knew Poppa would approve of the color. I added a short strand of pearls that Tom had given me. My father being a Southern gentleman did his best to put him at ease, at least at first.

Some of the colored waiters, who had worked there before the war, were still there. Several of them remembered my father and they seemed delighted to see him. Poppa even called several of them by name.

We had a venison roast with potatoes and carrots, fried eggplant, fruit compote that had been marinated in Brandy. We drank a lot of wine, too.

After supper, I still can't call it dinner, the northern term, Poppa grew very quiet and said. "Thomas, as a lawyer you know that marriage is a legal contract."

I held my breath; I was afraid of what would happen next.

"Couples may marry in church, but they divorce at the Courthouse"

Thomas' face flushed. "I have no intention of divorcing your daughter," Tom said emphatically!

"I didn't think for one minute that you would." Said Poppa

"However Mary Margaret's mother and I would very much appreciate it if you would agree to have your marriage blessed by an Episcopal priest."

"Oh, Yes, I would like that." quickly replied Tom.

"Maggie, can you arrange for that to happen while your father is still in town?" Tom asked.

There was a long silence. Then I realized I had stopped breathing.

"Poppa, I don't know of an Episcopal priest who would bless our marriage"

"What do you mean?" Poppa said with a frown on his face.

"Poppa, Thomas and I were never allowed to attend the church in Van Buren. People hated him because he was the last Union General in town."

"Were all the churches the same?"

"As far as I know, I wasn't interested in any other."

Poppa lowered his head and mused, "Jesus forgave, why can't people?"

"Thomas, are you an Episcopalian, too?"

"No, Sir. I am not. I am not a member of any church, currently"

"Then you have been baptized?"

"Yes, I was baptized in the Roman Catholic Church in Iowa." He relied. "But I have fallen away from its teachings."

Poppa very kindly said "Well at least, you have been baptized. I'll pray that someday Mary Margaret will lead you into fellowship of the Episcopal Church. There is a rumor that the House of Bishops is sending a Northern Bishop down to Arkansas. Maybe things will be different then."

I breathed a premature sigh of relief.

My father's tone of voice took a different turn, "I guess Thomas got elected to the Constitutional Convention because most of the Democrats couldn't vote." Poppa had had too much wine was my first thought.

"Poppa, Thomas is a wonderful man, and served in the Iowa Legislature before the war. He has a lot to offer to this state, as do other delegates.

"I am so sorry, it's not the kind of topic one should discuss at dinner. I didn't mean to spoil it.

"I came down here to see my beautiful daughter, not bring up past events and hurts. I'm going to order champagne to celebrate your marriage and my getting to meet my son-in-law."

A number of the delegates were dining there that night and I was pleased to introduce my father as Dr. Richard Thompson. Another one of delegates was Powell Clayton, who later became Governor, and his wife Camilla. His brother was with them. He has a long name: William Henry Harrison Clayton. I guess that was no worse than people naming their sons after George Washington or Thomas Jefferson. I wondered why his parents named him after that President, but I didn't ask. I was delighted that Poppa got meet them. At one time Poppa considered them enemies, but I was glad he could meet them as just men.

Poppa said that before he left for home he would like to see Sandy Faulkner. "I would love to hear him sing and play 'The Arkansas Traveler' one more time"

Tom said, "Mr. Faulkner has a house in the third block of Broadway, but it would be easier for you to see him at the Capitol. Mr. Faulkner has fallen on hard times, and we have hired him as Door Keeper for the Convention"

"Poor Sandy, he never could hold on to his money. I won't stop by to see him. Seeing me might embarrass him."

"Well dear children, the evening is getting late for an old man."

"Don't say you are old, Poppa"

"You can't fool Father Time." Poppa answered

As we parted Poppa shook Thomas' hand and hugged me, and said how glad he was to see me and meet Tom. It would be several years before I saw my father again.

I learned later that night that Tom had to be baptized in the Roman Catholic Church before Eleanor's parents would let them marry. That was as big a farce as the marriage was. I actually thought that taking baptismal vows you really didn't mean, was bordering on a major sin.

"Maggie, would you like for me to join the Episcopal Church?"

"Only if you really want to, Tom."

"You know I would do anything to please you."

"I don't want you to join for just that reason."

"Maggie, I don't really know what Episcopalians believe."

19

"Don't worry, many of them don't either. We'll talk about it another time. Maybe the new Bishop can talk to you about it. This has been a trying day, and I just want to go to bed."

We didn't make love that night. Poppa had cast a pall of gloom over everything I loved. I hoped I never saw him again.

CHAPTER 4

NEW FOUND FRIENDS

Just as former Yankee soldiers were not welcome in Arkansas, especially if they were married to southern girls, neither were their wives. The wives of the delegates who had believed in the Confederacy never invited any of us "Yankee wives" to social gatherings.

On day I was walking down Broadway and approaching me were four "Southern Belles" in their slightly out-of-date hooped skirts. When it became clear that they were not going to let me pass, I just stepped off the curb into the street and kept walking in the opposite direction. One of them actually spit on me as I passed and another one called me a "traitor". I cried all the way home. My eyes were still puffy when Tom got home, and he asked why. I told him about how the Southern girls treated me. "Mary Margaret," when he called me by my full name I knew he was about to say something I had better pay attention to. "The South lost the war and they need to get over it, although I doubt if they ever will. Just ignore anyone who is so immature."

I finally found three other Southern girls who had also married Northern boys who were connected to the convention. What a relief to find them. The Southern girls who had married Southern boys distanced themselves from us, and sometimes were just plain rude. So much for Southern graciousness. I was sure it wasn't thoughtless rudeness, like the colonel's wife was at Ft. Gibson when we eloped. I always thought she did it on purpose.

Apparently, the Southern girls felt that we had betrayed the "Cause" by not marrying a Southern boy. I had several proposals of marriage to local boys before, and at the beginning of the war. I found those nice young men to be boring. I believed that looking across the breakfast table at Tom Harwell, for the next thirty years was the most natural thing in the world. I will have to admit that later in life, boring might not have been too bad. Nothing could ever stop my loving Tom, and my love never wavered although I did stray once.

Camilla Clayton, Sue Sarber, Agnes Harrison and I would get together once a week to visit and not feel so left out of social things. We took turns being the hostess, and at whoever's house we met, the hostess would tell how she met and married her husband. We drew straws to see who would go first. Sue got the short straw, so we began our meeting at her house. They lived on Seventh Street. I didn't mind the walk however. Sue served the most delicious chocolate cake. None of us acted like ladies eating it. Chocolate had been so scare during the war, we were delighted to have it again.

Sue began her story: "My sister Frances and I rolled bandages for the wounded soldiers, every day. We would take them to the Presbyterian Church which was being used as a hospital. The church was pretty much just out our back door. I always carried my autograph book and had the soldiers, who were able, to sign it. Since my hometown of Clarksville changed hands so many times, there was often a mixture of Union and Confederate Soldiers there in the hospital. Regardless of which side they were fighting for, they all bled red blood."

"Did they cause trouble with each other since they were on opposite sides?" asked Agnes.

"Rarely" Sue continued. "They were generally too sick, or wounded, to stir up trouble with anyone.

"Did you help nurse them?" Camilla inquired.

"No, we just took bandages. Sometimes we would write letters home for them. One day I saw this handsome young Union soldier at the hospital. He wasn't wounded, but had come to check on the wounded men in the 2nd Kansas. He was the standing orderly for Colonel Cloud who commanded the 2nd Kansas Cavalry. I asked him to sign my autograph book which he did. When I looked into his clear blue eyes, I nearly swooned. It was John of course. He asked my name and that was it. I didn't think I would ever see him again. Shortly thereafter the 2nd Kansas pulled out of Clarksville and burned the Methodist Church that they had been using as a commissary."

"How terrible! A church?" I asked. The Northern branch of the church vacated all the Methodist pulpits in the South, and the building was no longer considered sacred by the Union Soldiers.

"My mother, sister and I, and a lot of other women and men who were able, rolled as many barrels of flour out of the burning building as we could, before the flames got too high, and the heat nearly overcame us. We spent that night making biscuits with that flour for the Confederate soldiers coming through town in pursuit of the 2nd Kansas.

"How on earth did you ever meet John again?" Everyone said in unison.

"I never dreamed I would see him again. I didn't really remember his name just his blue eyes. One day after the war, John, in a suit and vest walked into my father's store and introduced himself. He asked if he could speak to me. My father was flabbergasted at his request. John told me later Daddy asked where he had met me. John explained he had only met me once at Church. John didn't elaborate which church or when. He stated that he had just moved to Clarksville and opened a law office near the Court House.

Daddy finally agreed and sent the stock clerk upstairs to get me. Daddy had built a two story brick building with his store and warehouse on the first floor. On the second floor we had our living quarters which were quite ample. It was the first brick building in Clarksville.

I couldn't imagine who could be calling on me. I went downstairs and really didn't recognize him in regular clothes. Then he spoke to me, and I saw those blue eyes, I recognized him but still could not remember his name.

Daddy said that we could sit on the bench on the front porch. It was one of the pews that had been saved when the church burned."

"How ironic" said Agnes.

"I sat at one end of the pew, and he sat on the other. My sister, Frances, was so curious as to who my gentleman caller was, she brought us lemonade.

John asked if he could come to see me every Saturday. I said he could and hoped Daddy wouldn't object. We sat on the front porch every Saturday for two months. I later realized that the reason Frances was so interested in serving us lemonade every Saturday, was so she could come downstairs and smile at A. C. Miller who worked in the store. She was sweet on him. And they are going to get married."

"Did you ever get any time alone?" Camilla asked.

"Not until the end of the second month. We had been holding hands at a distance for a long time. One Saturday, Daddy had to go to some meeting about the railroad coming to Clarksville. He left A. C. Miller in charge of the store. John and I stood up and went for a stroll around the building and then went into the warehouse area, which can't be seen directly from the store. John grabbed me and kissed me, and I kissed back. We continued kissing until it wasn't safe for us to be gone from the front porch any longer. John asked if I would marry him. Of course I said "yes," but I told him he would have to get Daddy's permission first."

That caused a frown on John's face. "Does he know I fought for the Union?"

"I haven't told him, and he is still mad you all burned our church."

"I promise you I wasn't one of the ones that pitched a burning torch into the building. Colonel Cloud and I had ridden on ahead, but the Colonel had given the order to burn the church. I am sorry it was your church, any church for that matter. I am a Methodist and my father is a lay-preacher back in Kansas. At least he was before he died."

We were safely seated on the front porch when Daddy got back from his meeting. The next morning at breakfast Daddy asked me if I knew that John had fought for the Union?

I couldn't lie about it and "Yes".

Daddy cleared his throat and said, "I want him to stop hanging around here."

"Why?" I asked. "The war is over."

"I don't care, I don't want you having anything to do with a Yankee soldier." My father said curtly.

"Today he is going to ask your permission to marry me."

"What?" Everyone at the breakfast table exclaimed.

"I have already told him I would marry him." I announced.

My father got up and left the room he was so upset. He seemed to be throwing things around from the noise in the next room. My mother just stared at me."

"If he were a woman we could say he was having a 'hissy fit" laughed Camilla.

"What unit was he with?" My mother asked timidly.

I took a really deep breathe. What could I say but that he was with the 2nd Kansas. "He was Colonel Cloud's standing orderly."

"My mother put her head on the table and the room was completely quiet. Mildred, our maid, stood like a statue with a pitcher of milk in her hands. She was afraid to move." It was as if the silence was moving up the walls in waves.

After Daddy had composed himself, he came back into the room, and said, "Do you love him?"

"Yes, very much. If you and mother would get to know him you'd see what a fine man he is. He's a lawyer and is going to run for office."

"Dog catcher?" piped up Andrew, my brother.

"No, for the Constitutional Convention, smart mouth".

"That means he probably will win since so many of us aren't allowed to vote." Daddy said curtly.

My sister made the mistake of saying "You could take the oath, and then you could vote."

That's when Daddy flew into a rage, and told Frances to leave the room.

After a few minutes, my mother said, "Moreau, we can't carry hatred of what happened around with us the rest of our lives. Let's meet this young man, before you say "No." There weren't a lot of acceptable young men left after the War. They had either died or had moved west. Mother pointed out that as a Republican, John could run for office. It could be a chance for Daddy to get back into political circles. It's always the women who are the practical ones.

Daddy sat for a long time and then said, "Sue, invite him to Sunday dinner." I was thrilled.

Much to my surprise, that afternoon Daddy went to John's office and asked him if he really had asked me to marry him. John answered, "Yes, I have and I would like your permission to do so." Daddy turned around and walked out.

I was right and of course they liked John. Things would change later on, though. Daddy finally gave his permission for us to marry, if not his blessing. Then we hit a snag. Rev. Gregory at the Methodist

Church refused to marry us since John had been with the unit that had torched the church."

"What happened? How did the preacher come around." Camilla asked.

"I didn't know this until later, but Daddy struck a deal with the minister. The church had been interested in acquiring a piece of land at the edge of town, for a cemetery. Daddy owned the land, and if Rev. Gregory would marry us, he'd agreed to sign over the land to the church. Daddy made John promise to return to Clarksville after the convention.

So we got married in a home ceremony. Very few of the relatives or friends, would come, but I didn't care. I was going to marry John, no one else."

"Good for you" exclaimed Agnes.

"Where did you spend you first night?" asked Camilla.

"John had rented a house and had his law office in the front part of the house and the living area was behind it." Sue didn't offer any details and we didn't ask.

"Then John was elected as a delegate from Johnson County to the Constitutional Convention, and we came to Little Rock. I know things like this aren't supposed to be talked about openly, but I was with child when we left for Little Rock. Because of the excitement of moving down here, being away from home for the first time, and the trip itself, I lost the baby."

"Oh, dear; how sad; we are so sorry; are you all right?" We all chimed in.

Tears were rolling down Sue's face, and we all gathered around her and hugged her. "Does your mother know?" I asked.

"No, you all and John are the only ones who know, other than the doctor. He said it was just the trip and the excitement that caused it. He was sure there would be other babies. I didn't tell my parents because I knew it would cause another uproar. They would blame John for it. If the news got out, tongues would wag all over Clarksville, and would say that John must have beaten me. There are some very vicious people in Clarksville."

We immediately turned the conversation around to cheerier topics. Sue refilled our coffee cups, and we chatted like only women can chat.

That night I asked Tom if he knew that the Sarber's had lost a baby since they arrive in Little Rock.

"No, why would I know something like that?"

"I thought maybe John had mentioned it to you.

"No, that's not the type of conversation men have. John asked for a personal leave day recently, but I didn't know why. It wasn't my place to ask. I am sorry about it though."

Tom hugged me close and said "I love you very much, and I am sorry I can never give you a child. Things just don't happen in life the way we would like for them to, sometimes"

"But the doctor did say there was one chance in a million, didn't he?" I asked.

"Yes"

"Well, we haven't hit the millionth mark yet, but we need to keep on trying"

Thomas laughed, scooped me up and took me to bed where we kept on working toward that one in a million chance.

The next week we met at Camilla Clayton's. She served Bakewell pudding. She had found the recipe in her great-grandmother's recipe collection. Camilla's husband had been a Union General. She was from Helena, and he didn't have troops in that area so we were curious how they met.

Camilla explained, "My father is the Captain of a paddle wheeler. He flew the Confederate flag, but ran supplies for the Union, when asked to. His attitude was that U.S. money was better than the Confederacy money, and he realized early on, the Confederacy wasn't going to win. I lived on the boat and had for most of my life. My mother died when I was ten. When the Captain, which is what I call him, was going to be carrying supplies, he had me stay at the Phillips' Hotel in Helena. The Captain threatened every Union officer who was staying there within an inch of his life if they touched a hair on my head. They all remained gentlemen. Powell had to come to Helena to take some of the pressure off Colonel Griggs, who led the 3rd Minnesota. Most of the troops in the field were sick with malaria and were thrilled when Powell showed up with a case of quinine.

So, Powell stayed at the Phillips' Hotel too. I am a big flirt and tease and most of the men were afraid of my father, so they wouldn't tease or flirt back. Powell wasn't afraid of the Captain. I would tease him, and we would end up running up and down the front and back stairs of the hotel. Sometimes he chased me, sometimes I chased him. At one point, Mr. Phillips asked my dad if I could behave in a more lady-like manner. The Captain pointed out to him I had been around rough boat men all my life, and knew how to take care of myself. He told Mr. Phillips as long as we were making enough noise so that everyone knew where we were then there was nothing to worry about.

One day, when I knew Mr. Phillips had gone to town, I let Powell catch me. We slipped into one of the upstairs rooms and hugged and kissed until we were out of breathe Then we lay down on the bed.

"Oh, you didn't", gasped Agnes

"Yes, we did, but we kept our clothes on. We heard Mr. Phillips come back, so we got up, and we went down separate stairs cases. I was still a virgin but I knew I didn't want to be one much longer."

"You wicked girl!" Agnes said blushingly.

"Finally the stupid war was over, and Powell came back to Arkansas after he mustered out. He bought a plantation at Swan Lake which is south of here. He came to Helena to get me, he said. He asked the Captain for my hand in marriage."

"Lord, yes. The sooner you take that girl off my hands the better." he replied.

"We got our wedding license the next day and got married immediately at the Court House. The Captain threw a big luncheon for us, and told us he was going to spend the night on the boat, and we could have his room. It was late afternoon before all the doings were over. We went straight to our room and didn't waste any time becoming man and wife."

"I can't believe you said that," murmured Agnes.

"Agnes, you need to grow up. We are all married women, and we know what marriage is really about, so put aside the Catholic girl innocence." said Camilla a gently as possible.

"I'm not used to people taking so openly about personal things" She replied.

"Most of us aren't either, but we are married women and are not the innocent virgins we once were." I pointed out. "We don't need to blab intimate details, but we all do know what goes into having a happy husband."

As the meeting was breaking up Agnes asked if I could stay a little longer, so I did. She confessed that she knew nothing about the marriage bed until her wedding night. She said that Chase was very kind and understanding, but she was not sure what proper behavior was for a wife.

"You and Tom have been married for three years, isn't that right?" Agnes asked.

"Yes, and they have been happy years.

"Do you all still? . . . you know . . ."

"Good Heavens yes! That's part of loving your husband." I exclaimed.

"Well, Sunday night is about the only time we . . . you know."

"You only make love once a week?"

"Yes."

"Child, if you love Chase, and want him to be a loving and faithful husband, it has to be more than that. Why just Sunday night?"

"My church teaches that we are giving in to our base animal instincts when we indulge in that activity."

"The Bible says to go forth and multiple. How did you think people do that?"

"Oh" said Agnes.

"And who made those rules? Virginal old men who have never known the joys of being with a woman, that's who!"

"I guess so."

"Agnes, is there some reason Chase is willing only on Sunday nights?"

"No, he would like more, but I thought it was wrong to do it so often. I thought couple conjoined only when they wanted to conceive a child. Plus I thought it wouldn't be such a sin since we had been to confession and church that day."

"Agnes, you need to make love to your husband every morning, every night and every time you can get him to drop his pants".

Agnes' eyes got big. "Really?"

"Yes, really! Otherwise he'll go find some whore to take care of his needs."

"Oh, no. I would just die if he did that" Agnes said with tears in her eyes.

"And, you need to enjoy being with your husband that way as much as possible, because he will enjoy it more too."

More big tears came up in her eyes. She hugged me and thanked me and told me what a good friend I was.

Two months later, Agnes came to our weekly visits with a big grin on her face.

"Ladies", she announced, "I am with child."

We congratulated her, hugged her and wished her well. Then Camilla made the same announcement. Sue then admitted she thought she might be. That worried me because it was so soon after she had lost a baby. My fears came to naught.

After the meeting, Agnes whispered to me softly. "I can't thank you enough, and neither can Chase."

"You told him what I said?" I couldn't believe it.

"Yes, and he said you were a very wise woman. He said that must be why Tom is always in a good mood—at least before some of the delegate start acting badly." Agnes reported.

I blushed that time. I told Tom about all of it that night and he stormed,

"Good God, Woman! Don't be babbling your mouth about our personal life. And don't be giving out instructions to other women."

"I didn't. I just told her what to do to keep Chase happy."

Tom drew his own conclusion.

"Did you tell her we came together before we were married?" asked Tom.

"I most certainly did not." I emphatically replied.

"I don't want you talking about that to any other friends. Do you understand me?" cautioned Tom.

"Yes, Agnes asked me for advice; I didn't seek her out"

Tom opened the back door, slammed it shut and went into the yard to smoke a cigar. He kept shaking his head. Tom's outburst really surprised me.

It was my turn next to have the weekly tea-party. I had Mrs. Hughes serve us southern tea-cakes and coffee. I was somehow embarrassed that I had maid. The other ladies didn't have household help.

We had just finished our coffee when my nose started dripping, and so I excused myself and opened the bedroom door so I could get a handkerchief. Agnes stood up and screamed and then collapsed onto the floor crying her eyes out. We were appalled and confused. What on earth was wrong with her? She actually had a light fainting spell, too, so we got her up onto the settee. She finally calmed down, and when she could speak she said, "That's my bed."

"Was your maiden name Abercrombie?" I asked. She nodded her head, yes. Then I realized how Mr. Derry could know all he did about the family who owned it. I didn't know what to say or do. We were all speechless. I fetched Mrs. Hughes and had her make more coffee.

Agnes then told the ladies the same story Mr. Derry had told me. She added that since she had no place else to go, she moved in with her mother's sister, Gloria O'Brien and a great aunt. "I was devastated when my father, mother and brother died. I had no place else to go but they took me in, although they had been at outs with my mother. They had not approved of her marriage. My father was a Protestant, and mother's family had been Catholic for a thousand years."

Agnes had an uncle who was a priest at Subiaco Abbey near Booneville, Arkansas. Aunt Gloria just couldn't believe her sister could love a Protestant.

I interjected, "Would you believe my father asked me if I married Thomas just so I could have enough to eat at the end of the war?" Men never understand the way of a woman's heart."

"The problem," added Camilla, "is that our fathers don't understand that we aren't little girls anymore."

In order to get Agnes calmed down, we asked her to tell us the story of how she met Chase.

"He was a member of the Union Navy and his ship was captured on the Mississippi River and he was taken prisoner. They took him to that terrible prison, on the hill, on the western edge of town. It is used now as a prison for common criminals. When Little Rock was captured, the U.S. soldiers released all of the Union prisoners. Since he was a practicing lawyer, he became the Solicitor General for the military courts."

"But how did you meet?" Sue asked.

"We are both Catholics, and I first saw him at church. He was hard not to miss. He's so tall and has such curly blonde hair. So I looked forward to church every Sunday hoping I would see him again. He was at Mass every Sunday too. One Sunday, after services, Chase was waiting at the bottom of the church steps, and asked my aunt if he might walk me home. She agreed, and I was thrilled. It was raining and he had an extra umbrella. He said he had been praying for a rainy Sunday so he could approach my Aunt and me. He walked me home every Sunday after that up to Easter Sunday. That day, my aunt invited him to have Easter dinner with us. We had the traditional lamb and ham and a lot of egg dishes. I was so pleased she invited him. He spent the afternoon entertaining us with stories about New York City. He and his brother had practiced law there before the war.

My aunt was so taken with him that she invited him to Sunday dinner the next week, too. After lunch, Chase and I sat in the swing on the front porch and just swung back and forth and held hands. He leaned over and kissed me right out there in the open. I was so surprised, but what surprised me more was that he got up and went into the house and asked my aunt if he could marry me. She gave a resounding "yes". I suspect my aunt would have let me marry anyone so that there would be one less mouth to feed. She really liked Chase and he was Catholic and a lawyer, so he fit all of her qualifications. Chase came back out and got down on one knee and asked me to marry him. I couldn't say "yes" quickly enough. We were married the next Sunday right after Mass. My Aunt had a really nice lunch for us at the Capitol Hotel and then we went upstairs to the room Chase had rented. I was such an innocent. Chase's patience was amazing, and we finally got the deed done. Then I was truly his wife. Chase said he would not have had it happen any differently."

The four of us were quiet for a time. She had told more than most of us expected, or needed to know.

Since my turn to be hostess that week turned out to be Agnes' story, when we met at her house the next week I got to tell my story. She served Juesites which was something new for all of us. It was obviously French. It was a pastry filled with pecan filling and they were exceptionally delicious. The pastry got its name because it was made into the same shape as the hats worn by the Jesuit priests. I knew nothing about them either. I didn't think it was my place to ask for an explanation, since I was an Episcopalian and had no need to know.

Then I told how I had met Thomas. "He had seen me once when I was downtown with mother. I had no idea he had even noticed me, although I got a glimpse of him and his shoulder length auburn hair and thought he was quite handsome. He wanted to meet me, so he asked our next door neighbor's wife have a tea and invite me and my mother. The family was Unionist and my mother did not want to go, but was afraid not to go for fear the Union soldiers would do something dreadful to us."

"At the tea, Thomas asked if he could call on me and I said, "Yes" before mother could say anything. The ladies there were shocked because I was so forward, but when I looked into those brown eyes I saw my future husband."

All my new friends sighed.

"Tom would come to see me every morning at ten o'clock. Mother was always fussing because he didn't know that in the South visitations were made in the afternoon. It was April and we were sitting the front porch swing. The trees across the entire valley were lacy with Spring. I loved that view, and it made me remember why I loved beautiful Arkansas so much. That day he got down on one knee and asked me to marry him. I jumped into his arms and kissed him. I know girls aren't supposed to kiss until they are married, but I just couldn't help it.

My father had abandoned my mother and me so he could go down to the Confederate State Capital in Washington, Arkansas because he thought he could serve the Confederacy better down there. Poppa was active in Democratic politics before the war. I knew my parents would never give me permission to marry a Union General. My father had left us; I didn't like my mother and didn't care what she thought, so I gave myself permission to marry him. We eloped to Fort Gibson in Indian Territory and were married by the Fort's Chaplain.

I'll never forget our wedding night, that's for sure."

The ladies stared at me in disbelief anticipating what I was going to tell.

"Oh, no Nothing like that. A terrible hurricane hit that night and we all had to take cover in the basement. It was just awful, and I was so afraid. If you have ever been in one, you'll never forget the sound of the wind that seemed to be blowing straight from Hell."

"Was the Fort damaged?" asked Sue.

"The roof was blown off the Officers' quarters, and one soldier broke his leg running downstairs. Some horses died when lightning hit the stable. We started back home the next morning because Tom was afraid the storm had hit his troops in Van Buren. Luckily, the storm had turned south a while after it hit the fort, and Van Buren had received only some hard rain."

"Was your mother relieved to see you?" Camilla asked

"She wasn't there. I had left her a note that we were eloping, and she got so mad she took Aunt Marie and Uncle Henry, our slaves, down to Washington, Arkansas. I'm sure Poppa got the tongue lashing of his life. No doubt she blamed Poppa for leaving us and that led to my marrying Thomas."

The four of us were so glad we had become friends. We continued to get together once a week until Camilla and Powell left for the nation's capital, and the Sarber's went back to Clarksville.

CHAPTER 5

WE LOST THE WAR BUT WE ARE NOT DEFEATED

One night there was a loud banging on our front door. Tom grabbed his rifle and ran to see what was wrong. When he opened the door, he saw a neighbor and behind him was a cross burning in our front yard. Tom raced out and used the butt of his rifle to knock the cross over. "god damn it, I'm sorry we didn't kill all of them."

It's a wonder he didn't catch his night shirt on fire. The neighbor who had sounded the alarm went back across the street and returned with a bucket of water. We always kept a bucket of water in the house at night, in case a spark from the fire place got loose. Tom grabbed it and that finished extinguishing the fire. The neighbor, whose name I have forgotten, offered to help Tom move the charred cross out into the street.

"NO", Tom said quite loudly. "I am going to leave it there for everyone to see whether they want to or not." Despite the commotion Tom had noticed that none of the other neighbors had come out to see what was going on, or to help. No one had even lighted a candle. Tom was as angry about that, as he was about the burning cross." He decided right then that we were moving to a different house farther away from the Capitol building.

I was just frantic and so upset I couldn't quit shaking and was crying my eyes out. I was terrified about the burning cross, but almost as upset that Tom had let his hatred of the Confederates show. Mrs. Hughes had heard the noise and then saw the glow from the fire and thought our house was on fire. She came running downstairs to see if we had gotten out safely. When she saw the house wasn't on fire, she got a blanket and wrapped me up in it, and then made tea.

I was still shaking so badly, when she brought the tea, I couldn't hold the cup, so Tom held the cup to my lips and had me sip it. I finally stopped shaking but didn't think I would be able to go to sleep for the rest of the night. Mrs. Hughes had some Laudanum and offered to give me a dose if Tom approved.

"Only this once!" Tom said sternly.

Mrs. Hughes dashed back to her apartment and got the drug. She filled a tablespoon full of the medicine and had me swallow it. It really did calm me down, and I was grateful for it.

"Why did they do such a thing to you? You ain't colored." Mrs. Hughes asked.

"Because today we are going to debate and vote on whether or not we will give black men the right to vote. It was a warning that it shouldn't pass." Tom explained.

"I thought the Southern states had to give colored men the right to vote before they could be allowed to rejoin the United States." I said.

"Yes, that's right", replied Tom. "But some folks don't care if Arkansas is readmitted to the Union."

"That doesn't make a lot of sense, whether one thinks colored men should vote or not. The South lost the war. Do some people think we can just be our own separate little country?" I asked.

"It doesn't make a lot of sense, but a lot of things nowadays don't make sense anyway" was Tom's answer.

"Are you all going to debate about letting women vote?"

"Now, Maggie, this just isn't the time to bring that up. Please!" Tom kept watch all night. I was drowsy from the medicine, and I went right to sleep. I realized later Tom was doing more thinking than watching.

The conclusion Tom had come to that night was that we were going to move, but in such a way, people would think we still lived in the cottage. He asked Mrs. Hughes to join us in the house, and asked her if she had a man who could stay with her at night, there in the cottage.

"Tom!" I chided.

Tom ignored me and said, "I want it to appear that we still live here, and that we haven't been intimidated by the cross burning.

After a brief pause, Mrs. Hughes said, "Yes, Mr. Overman could stay with me."

I was taken aback. I didn't know her night time activities still included entertaining men.

"Tell me about Mr. Overman" Tom asked.

"Samuel is a tailor" she answered.

"Oh, I know him. He fitted me for a suit recently. He was in the 2nd Kansas wasn't he?"

"Yes, I think so."

"John Sarber recommended him to me. That would be fine with me, if he agrees." said Tom.

She didn't answer immediately, but said that she was sure he would agree. "He often spends the night with me." Tom didn't seem shocked. I was, maybe just because I didn't know of it.

My next thought was: Not in our bed, you won't.

Tom must have read my mind because he said, "Is the bed in your apartment large enough or do I need to get you a different bed."

"No, that one has been just fine for us" she said with a slight blush on her cheeks.

"Once we get our furniture moved, then we'll move your bed into this house."

Tom instructed, "I want you and Samuel to keep all the drapes closed tightly at night but keep the candles lit until it time to go to bed, and then blow them out. I want people to think we are still living here."

I thought, I bet they don't wait until the candles are out, I know we don't.

"Does Samuel have a gun-'er a rifle?"

"I assume he does."

"If he doesn't have a rifle, I'll buy him one. He is to keep it loaded and close at hand at all times. I am also giving him permission to use it when necessary."

Of course I couldn't say anything, but I was sure Mr. Overman had a gun that he fired into Mr. Hughes every night. It really wasn't any of my business; I think I was just irritated because I didn't know it was happening out our back door.

"General Harwell, I want you to know that Mr. Overman and me plan to get married."

"Mrs. Hughes, that is your business and not mine. Don't feel that you have to marry in order to protect the house at night."

"Uh, no, sir."

"I'll come in through the alley, and go out the front door every morning just like I have been doing. Mrs. Hughes, I want you to go about your chores like you have been every day."

"I think we can pull this off. At least we are going to give it a try. We'll see what happens after the convention is over and what we'll do then."

Tom bought a house out in the south west part of Little Rock. It was almost at the edge of town near Mount Holly Cemetery. He had finally found out who had owned it through deeds at the Court House. He tracked them down and paid them for the house. They had moved to Texas, and wrote back how pleased and surprised they were that he hadn't just take the house since they had abandoned it.

Tom drove me out to our new house. The family who had lived there before, left a number of large pieces of furniture. We surmised they took what they could fit in a covered wagon. All of the rooms were larger and there was a formal parlor in the front of the house and a smaller sitting room upstairs at the rear of the house. A lovely flight of stairs led up to three bedrooms. Tom suggested I use the north bedroom for my painting studio. The kitchen was separated from the house by a brick walkway with grape vines hanging from the trellis work.

It suddenly dawned on me, I wouldn't have Mrs. Hughes to help me.

Tom must have read my mind because he said "We'll find someone to help you. Some of the colored men in town fought with the 2nd Kansas Colored. You know the one Sam Crawford commanded before he became Governor of Kansas. I'll check around and some of them surely have family with them now. Don't fret!"

I had loved our little cottage, but this was a really nice house and the prettiest carved mantel I had seen in Little Rock. It was a series of hunting scenes. It was very unique.

Tom devised a plan where a piece of furniture or two at a time was taken to the new house. Mr. Derry would use his covered delivery wagon to take them to the new house. I insisted that our bed and my piano be moved first. Getting the piano tuned after it got moved again would present a problem since our being there was supposed to be a secret.

Tom had me come into town with him until he could find a housekeeper because he didn't want me to be out there by myself.

It was the last day we were to be in the cottage that I loved, so I decided, despite the heavy gray clouds, to go to Morning Prayer. Our new house was several miles away so this was probably my last chance to go to church so easily. When I came out of the church after the service was over, the snow was coming down in sheets whipped by a strong wind. Thank goodness the cottage is so close, I was thinking when two men in dark clothes appeared out of the snow storm and grabbed me and threw me into the back of a covered delivery wagon. "What are you doing?" I barked "I'm Mrs. Thomas Harwell and my husband" . . . . at that point, one of the men crammed a smelly rag into my mouth.

"Oh, we know who you are" they laughed, heartily.

The wagon was already underway, and the man who wasn't driving, pulled a small pistol from his jacket pocket and aimed it at me. I froze, which was probably the reaction they wanted.

"Look at those big blue eyes, Charlie." Do you think those eyes get that big when her naked husband heads towards her to get his due?"

How vulgar! What was I going to do? I thought.

"Lay still" the man shouted at me. I was still trying to get free, although I don't know what I would have done, if I had managed to get free. He slapped me hard across the face. My face had never been touched in anger, and I started to cry. "Save your tears for later when you really do hurt. I bet I'm twice the size of your skinny butted husband. You are going to find out what a real man is like" he said.

I could tell the wagon was going up a slight slope and then it came to an abrupt stop. I suddenly became very afraid. I had never been this frighten during the war. Early in the war, I didn't have Tom to protect me. Tom got to Van Buren after General Blunt had done as much damage as he could. The fact that the Garver's lived on one side of my parents' house and they always flew the American flag may have helped keep us safe. On the other side was Jesse Turner, a lawyer, who was pro-Union, so I guess the Yankees must have thought we were, too. I was trying to keep my mind busy and off what was about to happen.

The men dragged me out of the wagon. Despite the heavy snow fall, I could see the dim outline of tomb stones. I thought they were going to kill me and bury me on the spot. One of the men held my arms and shoulders down hard on the ground, the other man was lifting my skirts and had started pulling down my undergarments when a pistol shot rang out, and the man fell dead on top of me. The other man ran off. I was screaming, but with the rag in my mouth the sound wasn't coming out. Then a tall thin man also dressed in black pulled the dead man off me and cast him to one side. He removed the rag from my mouth, and said, "Mrs. Harwell, I am in the employ of your husband I'll take you home."

He introduced himself as Mr. Sullivan, and said he was a Pinkerton detective. I was crying and shaking and, when we got to our cottage, he picked me up and pushed open the front door which I hadn't locked when I left for church. Mrs. Hughes jumped back in horror. Mr. Sullivan told Mrs. Hughes to get me a cup of tea, and he was going to find a boy to run and tell my husband what had happened.

"Oh, no, don't bother him. They are so busy at the convention." I said.

"Mrs. Harwell I am paid to take care of you, and if I don't get word to General Harwell, I will lose my job." He said as he went out the front door.

"General Harwell." I said out loud. I didn't heard Tom called that much any more.

When Mr. Sullivan came back into the house, I was sitting at the dining room table trying to stop acting like a ninny. Mrs. Hughes had wrapped me in a thick blanket, but I was still shaking. She took soap and water and tried to wash the dead man's blood from my face and hair. I had vomited on the way home so everything, including me, was a mess. In a few minutes we heard the muffled sound of a horse galloping through the snow in our direction.

Tom burst through the door. As he knelt and put his arms around me I started crying again.

"General, I'll be going now, and finish the matter," said Mr. Sullivan.

"Thank you Mr. Sullivan, I'll need your report later." Tom replied

"Yes, sir." And he was out the door.

Tom kept saying, "I love you so much. If anything ever happened to you, I don't know what I would do. You have been my salvation. After the ordeal with Eleanor I didn't think I could ever love, until I met you."

I started crying again. I had been crying so hard for so long, that I had given myself the hiccups. My trying to talk with the constant hiccups was funny, and we all ended up laughing.

Mrs. Hughes announced she was going to fix us a special supper that night. The snow storm was too bad to go out anyway. She fixed smothered chicken, mashed potatoes and yeast dinner rolls. She said I needed soft food on my stomach after the scare I had had.

Tom stayed home with me the rest of the day. He said that he told John Saber to act as *President pro temp* in his absence, and if John didn't have enough sense to adjourn for the day, they could all just get snow bound as far as he cared.

I slept most of the afternoon and after supper, I asked Tom what Mr. Sullivan meant that he worked for him.

"I hired him to protect you." answered Tom.

"Why do I need protecting?"

"Have you already forgotten what happened this morning?"

"No, why did they try to do that?" I asked, puzzled.

"They were trying to hurt me by hurting you?"

I teared up again. "So much hate, and what good does it do?"

Later that night, I asked Tom what he would have done if the men had raped me.

"I would find them and kill them." Tom said defiantly.

"Kill them?"

"Yes"

"Would you be able to kill another man?" I asked solemnly.

Tom just stared at me for a long time. Then he said, "Mary Margaret, I was in the war, of course, I have killed men. I didn't get to be a General by staying in a tent."

I started shaking again. How dumb could I be? I just couldn't imagine my dear, sweet Thomas killing someone. I had only seen him angry on a couple of occasions. I just couldn't believe there was a killer inside him, but the war was over, or so I thought. The war was not over for some people and probably never would be.

I just couldn't imagine my wonderful Tom being a killer under any circumstance, but, of course, he fought in the war and could have been killed himself. That night I slept in Tom's arms all night. He would not turn loose of me.

The next day there was a report in the newspaper about a man who had been found in Mount Holly Cemetery shot once in the back of the head. His body had been placed on the grave of a David Dodd, whom the Yankees had hung as a spy. Another man had been found with his head under water in Rock Creek. The newspaper editor theorized the man had lost his way in the snow storm, had tripped and fallen into the creek and drowned. I doubted if the man's drowning had been an accident. The paper said neither man had any identification, but they were wearing Confederate belt buckles. Neither Tom nor I discussed it.

Tom located a man who had fought in the 2nd Kansas Colored who had moved his family to Little Rock. Tom said the 2nd Kansas Colored had fought at the Battle of Jenkins Ferry in south Arkansas, and many of the men decided Arkansas was too beautiful to leave.

The man, Leroy Smith, had a sixteen year old daughter whom Tom hired to stay with me during the day and do light housekeeping. He didn't want me out there on the edge of town by myself and I didn't want to go into town every day.

Leroy's daughter was named Cassie and she was a sweet tempered person. One day, after about a month, I noticed she had put on weight in the middle and asked her if she was with child.

"Oh, yes mam. My boyfriend Jeremy just loves doing it, and we do it as often as possible. Then, all of a sudden, up pops this baby."

"What do your parents think about the baby?"

"They are tickled and relieved."

"Relieved?"

"Yes, Mam, they was afraid I weren't ever going to have a baby. I did it the first time when I was fourteen. My white master was the first one to show me how."

"Oh, I am so sorry." I said, trying not to sound as shocked as I was.

"Don't be. He gave me a pretty new petticoat. In fact he gave me something nice every time he came to visit me after dark."

"But I never got no baby. After Daddy went to fight, my mother and me went to Kansas to hide out. I kept a boy company there in Kansas, but he went out and got himself captured by the slave hunters. I never heared from him again. Still no baby. My parents were getting worried. I was sixteen by then and should 'a had at least one child"

"After we moved to Little Rock, Jeremy and me met and fell in love the very first time."

"Are you going to get married? I asked.

"No 'mam. Don't seem to be no point to it now. A Marriage License costs two dollars and we need the money for the baby."

I would have been glad to give them money for a license.

"My Maw and Pa jumped the broom twenty years ago and worked out just fine."

"Are you and Jeremy going to jump the broom?

"Probably after the baby comes, but jumping it now might make the baby come too soon."

"Cassie, I have a bad headache and I am going upstairs and lie down. Why don't you make some coffee for when I get up."

I went upstairs and put a cool cloth on my head and lay down. It is another culture, I kept telling myself. I also was envious that she was unmarried but with child, and I was married and would never have a child. I knew there would be no children, short of a miracle, when I married Tom but sometimes I just couldn't help but feel sad.

Tom came home and realized I had been crying. When I told him what all Cassie had said, he hugged me tenderly and then told me to get dressed in my finest because we were going down to the hotel for supper. He knew that would cheer me up, and it did. On our way to dinner, Tom cautioned me not to be judgmental of Cassie; that the slaves had to make their lives as best they could and many lived under terrible conditions. "I know that you and your family never would mistreat Marie and Henry, but not all families were that way. We heard and saw some really bad things in connection with the salves as we fought south."

Tom knew I wouldn't make a scene in public, so he told me that the question about whether women should be allowed to vote was brought to the floor of the convention. Initially I was thrilled.

"Did you put up the question for the convention?" I asked.

"No, Jess Cypert introduced the bill, but the hall was filled with boos and catcalls. One delegate said now we knew who worn the pants in Jess' family. One delegate moved that we take away the vote from all men and just let women vote." explained Tom

"What asses" I replied. "How did the vote go?"

"It never got to a vote, there was so much noise in the room. I excused myself from presiding, and so Sarber took over. To get the situation under control he moved to lay the subject on the table. The whole convention erupted in laughter."

"John said to lay the subject on the table, not the motion, right? And all the men knew what he meant, right?" I asked.

"Yes, how do you know so much about procedure?" asked Tom.

"Poppa was in the legislature, remember. Just wait until I tell Sue Sarber about what he said" I proclaimed.

"You will do no such thing!" Tom said pointedly.

"Why not?" I retorted.

"You don't need to be stirring up trouble in someone else's marriage" answered Tom.

"Well, I'm not going to speak to any of the delegates ever again." I said

"Do as you please about speaking to them, but I can guarantee you that none of them will care. Most men don't care what women think anyway"

'You'd better care what I think."

"I laid you on the table once as I recall"

"Yes, and it hurt my back."

"My back hurt the next day, too."

"Why, you had your feet on the floor, and you were standing up?"

"My back got a lot of action as I remember it."

"You weren't complaining at the time."

"Mrs. Harwell, I think it is time I took you home and reminded you who wears the pants in this family . . . at least until I take them off."

"Dinner first" I insisted.

After dinner we went home and continued our conversation. While we talked, Tom began getting undressed and was now lying on the bed buck naked.

"Maggie, why don't you bring that passion to bed and help with this situation that has arisen. You know it will really hurt if it goes down by itself."

"I have never believed that. If it would hurt going down, why doesn't it hurt going up."

"Maggie, get yourself into this bed."

"Yes sir, General Harwell, at your service."

He wanted passion that night, well, he got plenty of that but I don't think it was the kind he wanted!

I was still mad the next morning.

CHAPTER 6

OUR MOVE TO WASHINGTON CITY

I never dreamed I would move to Washington City, either. I was excited about moving, for a change. For a girl from Van Buren Arkansas, Washington City was as far away as the dark side of the moon, and just as mysterious. Tom laughed at me. He had been to Washington several times. Not just as a Union General, but in 1864 he was there with his natural father, James Lane when Tom was elected as a delegate from Kansas to the National Republican Convention. It was actually held in Baltimore but Tom stayed a week extra and visited Washington and the war department. He wanted to remind them that the war was being fought on the Frontier as well as on the east side of the Mississippi River. I never have understood how Tom, who was not in Kansas at that time, got elected from that state just as I could never understand how Samuel Crawford could be elected Governor of Kansas while he was commanding the 2nd Kansas Colored in Fort Smith, Arkansas. Politics in Kansas must be different than politics in Arkansas.

Seeing the nation's Capitol building for the first time took my breathe away. It was so large. As far as being beautiful, our Arkansas State Capitol had it beat.

The reason we moved to Washington was because Governor, now Senator Clayton, was in trouble with the Senate. They wanted to impeach him because apparently they had nothing better to do. As Governor, he had done some things in Arkansas, after being elected a Senator, that upset some men in both parties. Powell did not like the Lt. Governor and did not want him to follow him as Governor, so he would not leave for Washington until a deal could be worked out. He

47

wanted the Lt. Governor and the Secretary of State to trade positions. It was an arrogant thing to do but it wasn't any business of the U.S. Congress' what states did in their own local politics, however Powell certainly made no friends. However, something else Governor Clayton did while still in office was the business of the U.S. Congress and the committee in charge of elections moved to have Powell impeached.

Thomas Boles was a lawyer from Danville, Arkansas. Unfortunately he was a Captain of Company E of the Third Regiment of Arkansas C.S.A., which displeased Powell but had nothing to do with the ensuing mess. There had been some tampering with the ballots in the Third Ward of Little Rock. Thomas Boles and James Edwards were running for US Representative. Powell prematurely issued a certificate of election to Boles. After all the mess was straightened out, Edwards had won the election by fifty votes but the certificate of election had already been issued. At this point, Congress decided to get involved. They drew up an eight hundred page indictment against Senator Clayton to try to impeach him.

Tom was asked to be his personal lawyer during the impeachment trail. He was delighted to be asked regardless of the circumstances.

The afternoon of the impeachment trial, Camilla and I sat next to each other in the visitor's' gallery and held each other's hand tightly. We were both anxious for our men. The Senate chamber was very intimidating.

I had never seen Tom in a court room before and, although I am his wife, I thought he was brilliant. The Senators must have thought so, too, as they acquitted Powell. Camilla and I wanted to scream for joy, but our southern rearing held strong and we remained ladies.

That night we celebrated by dining at Harvey's and Holdens restaurant, We feasted on oysters and consumed way too much champagne. The next morning's headache was a small penalty for such a grand victory.

CHAPTER 7

WASHINGTON TO IDAHO

The next week, Tom burst into the hotel room with a big grin on his face; picked me up and whirled me around until I was dizzy.

"What has come over you?" I stuttered.

"Mary Margaret I received a telegraph from President Grant, and he has appointed me Governor of Idaho Territory."

"Why a telegraph? We are right here in Washington."

"That's the way it is officially done."

"Idaho Territory; is that a part of the United States?"

"Yes, my love, it is, and as soon as enough people settle there, it will be a state just like all the other states." said Tom. "Kansas was a territory first and then a state, just like Arkansas."

"Where on earth is it? Is it beyond Kansas?" I knew where Kansas was.

"It is quite a distance from Kansas. It is north of Utah territory, and it borders on Canada."

"Canada, that's a foreign country! Do they have Indians, too? It might as well be on the other side of the moon as far as I am concerned."

Tom was exuberant. "Little did I realize ten years ago when I met General Grant in St. Louis, that he would become President of the United States, or that I would be appointed a governor."

"You weren't a General then, were you?"

"No, and he was only a Major. Lincoln had just ordered him east to try to get the war to come to an end." said Tom.

"How does one even get to Idaho?"

"I don't have the exact route yet." said Tom.

"How soon do we have to leave?" I asked begrudgingly.

"I thought I would go out first by myself and check everything out, get settled and then send for me?"

"Send for me like a package?"

Tom ignored me.

"How long will it take you to get there," I asked pointedly.

Several weeks I am sure, maybe more. Remember what Horace Greely said, 'Go West young man, Go West!'"

"Yes, but he said nothing about taking women with them. You are going to go off and leave me, just like Poppa did during the war. Is this your way of abandoning me?"

"God damn it, Maggie, if I thought it was all right to hit a woman, I would be sorely tempted right now. It's just until I get settled, then I'll send for you to come." said Tom.

"You expect me to travel alone all over God's green earth to get to some place called Idaho all by myself?"

"I hadn't got that far in my thinking, but surely we can find a travelling companion for you."

"So, two unescorted women will travel alone across the wilderness? My traveling with a strange man would certainly not be acceptable." I pointed out.

"Maybe we can find a missionary family who will be going west to start a mission, and you could travel with them." suggested Tom.

"You can be sure it won't be an Episcopal family. They have enough sense not to go into places where there aren't many people, most of whom can't read or write."

"That never stopped the Catholics." said Tom

"Well, hooray for the Pope! The priests don't marry anyway so they don't have to be responsible for women."

"I could probably hitch a ride with a Mormon family, they might be needing another wife" I said sarcastically, "it seems as if thousands of them are trekking west."

"No, you will not go with the Mormons, and don't mention it again. Do you want an armed escort of U.S. soldiers to escort you? It probably could be arranged because of my position and influence around army circles."

"Maybe I won't go at all!"

"Maggie, you always said you would be happy as long as you were with me.

"That's my point exactly, I won't be with you, and you may get killed and I'll never see you again."

"I made it through the war, Confederates were scarier than Indians, trust me. Maggie, can't you be happy for us?"

"I can be happy for you, but not for me. You won't need me once you get to Idaho." I pouted.

"What do you think you are going to do, go to a convent? Maybe you can go to the same one as Eleanor." He said sarcastically.

"She's Catholic, so it won't be the same one. I could go to the Episcopal convent in Baltimore, however".

Tom was really getting angry by then. I just sat down on the bed and could not feel good about any of it.

"Maggie we have friends here, and I'll see that you are well taken care of. It's not going to be forever. Plus you have been wishing you had more time to paint."

I sat there sullenly.

"For heaven's sake, Maggie, you are going to be a Governor's wife. Can't you be happy for us? Now I won't have to depend solely on winning at poker to support us. They say there is a fortune to be made in mining out there. The Governor's pay starts immediately. You'll have plenty of money while I'm gone.

Please stop pouting and put on your prettiest evening dress. We are going to celebrate tonight!" Tom insisted.

I got dressed to go out while not saying one word to Tom. Why can't they get a bachelor to go wander off into the wilderness to get killed, I thought. I don't want to be dragged through a thousand miles of dirt and dust and possibly wild Indians just so he could be Governor. I didn't give two cents about being called a Governor's wife. If that is being selfish, that's just the way it is.

"I guess there are enough loose women between here and Idaho to take care of you manly needs?"

"Maggie, I have never been unfaithful to you. Why would I start being unfaithful to you now?"

"Because, I won't be there to meet your needs. I always saw to it that you were well satisfied at home."

"Are you telling me that you made love to me just because you had to? It seemed to me that you thoroughly enjoyed it."

"No, I loved having you on me and in me. But, do you think you can do without making love for several months?"

"The same goes for you, Maggie"

"No, it doesn't. I don't know of any brothels for women that will serve their needs, as you always called it. Maybe you can find a Mrs. Hughes to take care of you while you are so far away."

"That not fair, Maggie. Men have a way of getting release without having a woman involved."

"Well, good for you! Maybe I can figure out some way to take care of my needs for love by myself." I replied

"Well, there are ways, but I have never bothered to show them to you because you always had me" answered Tom.

"Again, that's my point. We will be separated, so we won't have each other to show each other physical love."

"There are other ways to show each other love. I have always tried to please you and make you happy, not just in bed" said Tom softly.

"Well, this doesn't make me happy nor does it make any sense either."

"Mary Margaret, I am going to Idaho, so just accept it. You want me to go to President Grant and tell him I can't accept this honor, because my wife doesn't want me to? If you want a divorce it can be arranged before I leave town. Then you can be the gay divorcee who can probably get her needs taken care of quite easily.

I raised my hand to slap him, but Tom grabbed my wrist and pulled me to him and kissed me quite firmly on the lips. I melted. "No, I don't want a divorce; I just don't want you to go to Idaho."

"Maggie, your choices are to join me in Idaho, or a divorce. That's the way it is. If you want a divorce we can take care of that before I leave."

We said virtually nothing to each other at dinner, but we were well mannered enough to exchange cordial words with people we barely knew. Tom was not in government, and Washington had a very closely knit social circle. It was the first time in my life I didn't feel as if I belonged.

After dinner, which I can't even remember eating, we went upstairs. All I wanted to do was go to sleep, and wake up tomorrow with Tom's having changed his mind. I wished Powell had never asked him to be his personal lawyer during his impeachment trial. Tom won the case; he is a good lawyer. The impeachment was a farce. It was a just case of political back biting. Why couldn't we just go home? We could go back to Van Buren and Tom could practice law, and I could give a few piano lessons. Blessedly, sleep came quickly.

The morning brought on no change in attitude on Tom's part or mine. I just wasn't going to go to some god-forsaken place. Tom started bringing out his "Carpetbagger" suit cases and a small trunk that we had brought with us to Washington.

"You are going to help me pack, aren't you?" asked Tom.

"Why don't you just wait and see what the latest fashion in Buckskin suits is." I replied.

"Mary Margaret if you can't be happy about my appointment then just be quiet about it. You have made your point perfectly clear. Go downstairs and eat breakfast."

"Maybe I can find a map that shows where Idaho is, or even if it is on the map. Maybe you could just follow Lewis and Clark's route." I said.

"Maggie, I had better hear that door close behind you in about a minute."

I left but I slammed the door hard enough it probably woke up every one on the floor. There was no point in my trying to get Tom to change his mind. As he said once, "Men don't care what women think". Husbands are the head of the house, and wives just have to submit to their decisions, but it doesn't mean a woman has to like it.

We hardly spoke to each other the rest of the week. Tom was busy getting everything ready to go, that included all the official letters and documents that he would have to show the officials in Idaho that he really was the new governor. Actually, Idaho had just become a territory so Tom would be the first governor of the newly formed territory. I spent a lot of time that week going shopping. I wasn't going to be left high and dry in Washington wearing last year's fashion.

For the first time in our marriage, we were not intimate once that week. The night before he left, he said, "I know that you don't want us to go to Idaho, but I do think it is the best thing for our future. I really can't leave without making love to you. You never have refused me and please don't start now. It would kill me."

I started sobbing. "I love you so much, and I am so afraid that something awful will happen to you. I couldn't go on without you. I welcomed his embrace and our night was filled with love.

I saw him off the next morning with tears streaming down my cheeks as the carriage pulled away.

CHAPTER 8

FALLEN WOMAN

So what to do to fill the lonely hours? I wrote at least once a week to Agnes Harrison and to Sue and John Sarber who were in Clarksville. They had just had a baby girl named Lucille, after John's mother who had died when John was twelve years old. Sue was happy there and she had family, which was a big help since John traveled a lot. He seemed to have his finger in every Republican pie. Sue did complain that they seem to be the only Republican family in town. Her sister, Frances, married A. C. Miller so I guess all those trips to bring Sue and John lemonade did the trick.

Camilla Clayton was here in Washington City and tried to include me in as many social things as she could. An unescorted woman is looked upon with disdain. The fact that my husband was the Governor of Idaho Territory impressed them as little as it did me. They probably didn't know where it was either.

I did spend a lot of hours painting. I first painted a picture of my parents' home with all the roses in bloom. In the spring the house appeared to be floating on a cloud of color. Then I painted, as best as I could remember, the Drennen House in Van Buren. John Drennen founded the village of Van Buren which was first called Phillip's landing. The Drennen house was a long white house that sat on the bluff overlooking the Arkansas River with the business part of town being up on the cliff that rose in front of the house. I tried to paint the stockade at Fort Gibson, but I kept getting upset about how rude the Colonel's wife had been to me. I guess I didn't have anything else worthwhile to think about, or I wouldn't bring that up. Then I would remember the terrible storm that hit the fort on our wedding night and I ended up crying just thinking about all of it.

The hotel was close enough to an Episcopal Church that I felt safe in going to Morning Prayer almost every day. I did meet one or two people who assumed I was a widow and were very solicitous about my well-being. They were still strangers, and I didn't volunteer too much information. It still pained me that Tom and I had never had our marriage blessed by an Episcopal priest. After church, I would go back to the hotel and have breakfast.

Tom had been gone about a month, and I was bored to tears. I was tired of painting and reading dozens of books from a near-by book store. I never felt safe about venturing very far away from the hotel. Some days I thought I would scream.

I did get an occasional wire from Tom saying how the trip was going. I doubted if he really told me the difficulty of the trip, because I didn't want to go to start with.

One day after Tom had been gone about six weeks, I decided I was going to rent a carriage and go to Georgetown. It was such a charming place, there on the edge of Washington City. I had read in the newspaper that a new art gallery was opening and that was as good an excuse to venture out as not. The ad had said that the gallery was going to specialize in showing works of new and unknown artists. They did have one of John Audubon's paintings and that would worth the trip in itself. Some of the paintings were breathe taking. I especially liked one painting by a Mr. Whistler, and another one by Winslow Homer. What a strange name. It must be a family name I thought. The painting by Audubon was of a swan and the detail was exquisite. Some of the others were no better than mine. None of the European Masters had works hanging there which disappointed me. But, it was great to be out of the hotel and could visit intelligently with the gallery owner.

There were so many charming shops, book nooks, needle work shops I was sorry I hadn't come to Georgetown sooner. I slipped into a small bistro to get a bite to eat. I was so tired of hotel food even though it had a highly rated restaurant. Unfortunately, I knew one of the men in the bistro. It was Senator Clay Landrieux the Senator from Mississippi. Camilla had introduced him to me at a reception. I wondered what he thought about my being out by myself.

To my surprise he was dismayed that I was eating by myself and asked if he might join me. He inquired after Tom and how he liked Idaho, and how soon I would be leaving to join him. All I could honestly say was that I didn't know the answer to either question. I knew he had arrived safely, or that is what he told me. I listened to Clay talk in that melodious southern accent that was so good to hear, instead of the harsh sounds of people from the North and East. I found that people from those regions were rude, too, at least by southern standards.

Senator Landrieux was a widower and said he liked to come to Georgetown to soak up some culture. That made me laugh. He, too, liked the art galleries and the quant book stores. He asked if I had dinner plans. Of course I didn't. He asked if I would do him the honor of dining with him that night. I agreed and hoped no one would see us and start a rumor or a scandal.

Clay, called for me at seven o'clock and we went to an elegant restaurant which, gratefully, had very low lighting. I didn't want to be seen out with a man I wasn't married to, although I had been glad to accept the invitation. After dinner, he called for his carriage, and escorted me back to my hotel. I told him how much I appreciated his thoughtfulness. He saw me to the elevator, bowed, kissed my hand and bid me good night. I was thrilled with the evening.

The next day I received a note from Clay, asking if he might accompany me to dinner again that night. I eagerly accepted the invitation. That evening we went to a restaurant called The Oval Room and had a delightful meal of Sirloin of Beef with cherry mustard sauce in addition to new potatoes and asparagus. Dessert was chocolate mousse. We consumed a bottle of champagne too. I had never been to so fine a restaurant. When we got back to the hotel, I asked Clay if he would like to come up for a night cap. I am sure in the back of my mind I knew what I was really asking. Clay probably did too, and accepted.

I poured him a whiskey and fixed myself a very large glass of wine. We chatted about Washington gossip, which I didn't know much about since I wasn't involved with Washington's social life. Then I poured refills. Almost immediately Clay had moved next to me on the settee and took me in his arms and was kissing me intently. I kissed back with enthusiasm. There was a lot of kissing and fondling. We were soon on the bed partially undressed, then totally undressed. I gasped as I saw the length and girth of his member.

"Don't worry, petty lady, Big John isn't going to hurt you; he is going to give you a lot of pleasure." Oh, and he did, too. Clay's love making was amazing. Tom was a wonderful lover, but his didn't come with a deep southern accent. When Clay finished, he lay on his side and stroked my long brown hair which I had let down when we came to bed. Then he said,

"Pretty lady, would you do me the honor of allowing me to enter you again?"

I didn't hesitate. I ended up embarrassing myself by enjoying it so much. When we were finished the second time, it was getting late and Clay needed to be going. He couldn't be seen leaving the hotel after midnight. He said he would make sure no one was in the hall when he opened the door, and would find a poker game downstairs which he would use an excuse as to why he was there.

He suggested tomorrow night that we just order from room service and start with soup, and then just have an entrée of my choosing. He said we could supply our own dessert. I smiled and agreed, and I will have to admit I was excited about the prospect of being in bed with him again.

I lay in the bed in a warm, satisfied reverie when a thought shot through my brain like a bullet. Clay had not used any kind of protection. Tom is the one who is sterile, not me. My God, what if I had conceived! I sat straight up in bed and broke out in a cold sweat. What was I going to do? Surely there was a colored midwife in the city would could get rid of it. I had heard they were good at that. I was aware there were home remedies women used, to try to get rid of a baby, but I had never bothered to learn what they were. I couldn't imagine I would ever need to know them.

How would I find one of those midwives? I might have to take Camilla into my confidence, but I knew she would be shocked or at least surprised. Growing up on a steam boat she probably had learned a lot of things about life that I had been sheltered from. I knelt down by the side of my bed and prayed fervently for forgiveness and confessed every sin I could think of in addition to the adultery. I didn't feel much better after doing that; perhaps a little calmer. If conception had taken place it was too late now to pray it wouldn't happened.

Just as I finished begging for forgiveness, there was a knock at the door. Oh, please don't let it be Clay. I know I wouldn't be able to deny him. I opened the door and much to my relief it was a courier with a telegram from Tom.

I HATE IDAHO *stop*

ARRIVING HOME TONIGHT *stop*

TOM

I collapsed onto the floor and cried and cried. I was saved! I thanked God that Tom was coming home, and if I had conceived it would be covered up by Tom's return. I sent to note to Clay telling him that Tom was arriving in Washington City that night. I was sure he would understand without explanation. The Senate was in session so that afternoon I went to the gallery above the Senate floor to make sure he was present that day. He saw me, lifted the note, and nodded "yes". I had to make sure he had received my note. I breathed sigh of relief, but my feelings of guilt were still very present.

I got home as fast as I could as my beloved Tom was coming home. That evening dinner, as ordered with no dessert, arrive about seven o'clock. About thirty minutes later Tom was home. I was wearing my prettiest night gown and matching robe. The minute he opened the door I jumped into his arms. He couldn't stop kissing me. Then he took off his overcoat, picked me up and took me to bed. Our food got cold, but we didn't care. I told him how sorry I was for the way I acted when he left, and that I had been so lonely without him. I didn't tell him about sinning with Clay. He said he had been lonely too, and missed me so much, and not just at bed time. That night we made up for his being gone six weeks.

CHAPTER 9

RETURN FROM IDAHO

The morning after Tom's return, we ordered breakfast, and then he said with a smile on his face, "We are going home!" Tom announced we were moving back to Little Rock and he was going to run for the U.S. Senate. After having observed the Senators in Washington, he thought he had more to offer to this country than many of them did. He truly believed some were simply buffoons whose vote could be easily bought.

Then it dawned on me Tom had sold both our houses. Thoughtful Tom had sent a wire to a contractor in Little Rock several weeks before he gave notice he was leaving Idaho, to start construction on a new two story brick house just off Lincoln Avenue. It would be on a hill over-looking the Arkansas River. Tom said he requested there be a balcony on the back of each floor of the house. That way I could watch the traffic on the river, and he would have a place to smoke his cigars in peace. I would not let him smoke those stinky things inside.

We had stored our furniture before we went to Washington City in anticipation of shipping it to Idaho, if Tom's appointment was approved by Congress. With it not having to be shipped any place, it should still be in good shape. At least we would have our own bed back! I think a couple's bed is most important piece of furniture in the house.

There was already a large house just up the hill from where ours was to be. I was floored when we got back to Little Rock to learn our neighbor was Camilla Clayton's father who had moved his steam boat business to the Arkansas River from Helena. Although he had sided with the Confederates he wasn't above letting the Union Navy use his ship to ferry supplies to their troops. Thus, the Unionists had no problem with his building in that neighborhood. A number of the State Legislators lived in that area, too, and the stupid southerners called it "robbers' row" which I found distasteful. I had been reared in a Confederate household, but I knew first-hand how many good things the Republicans were doing for the state. I love Arkansas dearly, but there was so much to do to improve the life of its people.

I supposed that Camilla's father, Capt. McGraw moved to Little Rock in order to be closer to his daughter, but the Claytons were in Washington since Powell was a U.S. Senator from Arkansas. The house was beautiful and had so many stained glass windows in it. I imagined that Capt. McGraw had planned for Camilla to have the house after his death.

All of that got me to thinking about who would take care of Tom and me when we got old. Since we couldn't have children there wouldn't be any grandchildren. Unbeknownst to me, Tom had set into motion an ingenious plan to take care of that problem. I didn't know about any of it until we moved to Colorado a number of years later.

Until our house was finished, we moved into the new Capitol Hotel. The Metropolitan Hotel had burned down while we were in Washington City. The Capitol Hotel had hired a chef from New Orleans and the food was even better than what we had feasted on in Washington.

I asked Tom if he was going to play poker every night like he did before, when we lived in a hotel. He said that he didn't know. He had missed me so much when he was in Idaho he didn't want to spend any more time away from me than was absolutely necessary. The reality was several weeks later he decided that he needed to play poker every night, because of the contacts he would need to make in order to curry their favor and would win the Senate seat. A lot of important men played poker at night at the Capitol Hotel and a Gentlemen's club. I made sure the Gentlemen's Club was really just a place the men could get away from their wives, once in a while, and not like the Gentlemen's Clubs in Washington that were simply brothels.

My belief was that if I kept Tom sufficiently entertained at home, he would have no need to go looking for female entertainment elsewhere. There was plenty of female entertainment about six blocks east of the hotel. I became suspicious when women with too much make up, and too much of their bosoms showing, would come into the hotel lobby. They were unescorted, but the man at the front desk seemed to know who they were. I would turn my head and pretend I hadn't seen anything. Tom just smiled at me as if he didn't know what I was doing.

"Why would a nice hotel like this allow those women to come to this hotel for that obvious purpose?" I asked Tom.

"Don't you remember how shocked you were when you observed young men coming and going from Mrs. Hughes' quarters?'

"Yes," I answered, "but the war is over."

"Yes, but you explained to me it was war time, and those men were far away from their wives."

"The war is over!"

"You are still the sweet naïve girl you were when I fell in love with." Thank God he didn't know about my sinning with Clay.

"Men have needs, sweetheart, whether there is a war on or not. It has always been that way. I thought you understood that, of maybe you had just forgotten."

"I have never forgotten your needs."

"No, I have the best wife in the world" said Tom.

"Yes, and I prove it every night, don't I"

"Do you realize how much that means to me?" questioned Tom.

"Tom, I love you so much, I always want to make sure you aren't sorry you married me."

"I can't believe you said that. I can't think of anyone else I would want to be married to."

I squeezed his hand under the table and said, "I'm ready to go up to our room." Tom understood what I really meant.

"I am more than ready to go up to our room, but, Maggie, don't go nosing around trying to find out who those women are taking care of."

"I don't want to know, that's for certain. You make them sound like doctors."

"Well, they are going to make those men feel better and cure what is ailing them." replied Tom.

"I think you have said enough for one night, Mr. Harwell."

One day, Tom decided we needed to make a trip to Van Buren to round up the Republicans and remind them who he was. Also, to remind them what all he had done for Van Buren, and the state when he served in the Constitutional Convention. So we went. I had gone with him to Van Buren once before, although I really didn't care to go now. I was sure I had no friends left there, and I wasn't eager to see my father. He had sent me a note saying he was going to be in Van Buren for two weeks and asked that I come see him. His new wife and children would not be with him, so I was more relaxed about going.

My mother had died while we were in Washington, so I couldn't attend the funeral. One afternoon Tom said we were going for a drive. We started up Cedar Hill, and I couldn't figure out why. Almost to the top of the hill, he pulled the horses over, and said, "Get Out." I think he was afraid I wouldn't. We were at Fairview Cemetery where my mother was buried. Poppa had put up a nice stone.

"Come on over here," Tom said. He took my hand and led me past several graves and then I saw it. It was the tombstone for our dear friend John McGinity. I fell to my knees and wept. I would never get over John's committing suicide because of that Confederate whore. I still believed the whole thing was our fault. We were the ones who introduced them.

The fateful night, he rode out of camp. No one knew where he was going or why. John had not asked Tom for permission to leave camp. He was distraught over learning that his lover was a Confederate spy and with child. John shot himself in the head. Hunters found the remains the next spring and buried him where he fell. Later, Tom and other soldiers paid for proper burial and headstone. The current cemetery grew up around John's grave.

"It wasn't our fault, sweetheart. None of us knew Carolyn was a Confederate spy against her will. She was trying to protect her grandfather." Tom reminded me.

"But you could have been killed when those boats were attacked, because of her treachery."

"But I wasn't" said Tom.

"It was just as well that their baby died." I commented.

Tom smiled as if he were keeping a secret. He knelt and put his arms around me and tried to comfort me. I think Tom's eyes got misty too; but men don't ever admit to crying. We stayed beside John's grave for a long time. Tom said that we needed to start down the hill before darkness fell. I thanked Tom for taking me to see Momma's and John's graves, but I was glad he hadn't told me in advance where we were going.

One really ugly thing happened while we were in Van Buren, the editor of the local newspaper renewed his attack upon Tom. Jake Cummings had hated Tom when he was the commanding officer in Van Buren, and was thrilled when we went to Little Rock. After our move to Washington City, he assumed we were gone for good. Our return surprised him, but he whipped into action and called Tom to task about the new State Constitution. He told as many lies about Tom and the State Legislature as *The Arkansas Gazette* did. Tom was just fed up with the whole thing. Some people just would not leave the past alone.

Tom announced one morning he was going to Fort Smith for the day. He did not invite me to go. He just said that he had some business to take care of. He took care of business all right. When he came back to Van Buren that night he has a black eye and some scrapes on his face. He and the local editor had agreed to meet at a certain time and a certain place in downtown Fort Smith. It was supposed to look as if they had just run into each other accidentally. Apparently half the men in town knew this was going to happen. A large crowd of men gathered around Tom and Jake Cummings and even place bets on who would win. I was appalled at the whole thing. Tom had been declared the winner and the editor didn't say anything else bad about Tom in the newspaper. *The Fort Smith New Era* even ran a story about it. I was glad we were Van Buren only for a short time.

While we were in Van Buren, I had no choice but to see Poppa. He had remarried at bit too, soon after Momma died, to suit me, but I remembered what it was like to be lonely even if it was just for six weeks. Everyone thought Poppa, a medical doctor, was going soft in the head when he gave up practicing medicine and started growing fruit trees. It was common knowledge that you couldn't grow apple, pears, plums trees in Arkansas. Poppa was determined to prove everyone wrong. Once he stopped buy starts from Yankee peddlers and searched the woods for trees that were trying hard to bear fruit he dug them up and planted them on his own land. The peddlers' fruit trees were right for northern soil, but not for Arkansas soil. It took him several years before he got it all figured out; just how much and what kind of fertilizer to us for each kind of tree. Then he couldn't grow fruit trees fast enough to supply everybody. Luckily he owned four thousand acres, so he had plenty of room to grow the trees. He got so successful at it that he ran an ad in the Arkansas Gazette, that he had 200,000 fruit trees and bushes for sale. People were amazed.

I was pleased that Poppa was on the very first faculty of Arkansas' new Industrial University at Fayetteville, Arkansas. He taught Horticulture. He was home for the summer break, but had left his new wife and her children in Fayetteville so I didn't have to pretend to be nice to them.

It pleased me too, that Sue Sarber's husband was the Legislator who introduced the bill that created the university. It passed without any problem. The former Union soldiers were appalled at the lack of schools in Arkansas. There were various private schools for the children of wealthy parents. One such school was the Wallace Institute in Van Buren. It was for boys only. Girls didn't need to know anything except how to set a fine table and entertain guest.

I am sad to say that many people in Arkansas, both adults and children could not read or write. You didn't need to know those things to work in the fields. I was fortunate in that Poppa could afford to send me to the local female school where we studied real subjects.

Nothing pleased me more than when the State Legislature created a public school system, too. Now, bright young women hold school until they got married. The pay wasn't much, but, at least, they had some experience with money instead of being a ninny like I had been. Women do know how to love, educated or not, and that is important for everybody.

Chapter 10

Race For The US Senate

I couldn't have been happier or more at peace in our new home, until one day Tom came in with a wide grin on his face and announced he had been asked to run for the U.S. Senate. I was horrified! I loved our house and I didn't care that much for Washington City to begin with.

I had mixed feelings about Tom's being elected to the U.S. Senate. We would live in Washington only about six months during the year, and then we'd be back in Little Rock. At least I could then go to all the elite teas and parties that the Senators wives were invited too and not feel so left out as before. I hoped I wouldn't have to see Clay very often. As it turned out he had given up his Senate seat so he could stay home and run his plantation and be with his twelve children. I knew his wife had died. I suspect it was from having twelve babies. I felt sure Clay kept her with child all the time. I bet she died just so she could stop having babies. I chastised myself for having such an ugly thought.

Just like boys fighting in the school yard, the members of the Republican Party started fighting amongst themselves. They split up into two different factions. One faction, whose leader was John Price called themselves the Minstrels because he once appeared in a minstrel show. I attended a minstrel show once with Tom, but refused to go to any others. I thought they were tasteless.

The other faction took the name the Brindles, because Joseph Brooks, its leader, had a voice like a brindle cow. I really think they could have found something else to call themselves in either case. Only men would come up with such names.

The Minstrels had asked Tom to run. His opponent for the U.S. Senate seat was Stephen Dorsey, a Brindle, who appeared on the scene unexpectedly. He was president of the Sandusky Tool and Iron Company and the Ohio Tool Company, and had been sent down from Ohio by some investors to take advantage of the railroad construction. He had never been to Arkansas and cared nothing about the state only about making money. I suddenly had the insight that that was exactly the way people in the South felt about the Union soldiers who stayed behind after the war. The former Union soldiers felt they were doing good but the populous saw them as nothing but intruders.

I had no doubt but that Tom would be elected. I was wrong. People who didn't like Tom, for whatever reason, came out of the woodwork, so to speak, as soon as the announcement was made. The Gazette led the charge against him. They made a big deal that he was divorced "and had broken the scared promise". Thank goodness they didn't know about the baby. Tom was not about to embarrass Eleanor by sharing the facts about their non-marriage. Even if he had told them that she was in a convent in Arkansas the editor would have made something awful about that too. Some people did not like that Tom had been Powell Clayton's personal attorney during Powell's Impeachment trial in the Senate. Tom won the Case.

People didn't like it that Powell wasn't forced out of the Senate. The People of Arkansas really hated Gov. Clayton because he had tried to make them behave and stop all the lawlessness. They just wanted to run wild and do as they pleased.

One day Tom was walking down 4th street in downtown Little Rock and the editor of the Gazette, William Woodruff Jr. happened to come out of a building about twenty feet ahead of him. Tom was so mad about all the lies the paper had printed about him, he picked up a brick and threw it at him. Fortunately or unfortunately, the brick missed William. He tuned around and saw Tom, scurried down the street and ducked into the newspaper office on the corner. The paper wasn't as harsh on Tom after that but it did no good. Dorsey won the election. Tom said the rumor around the Capitol was that some Senators suddenly had a lot more money than before.

———◆◆◆———

One evening Tom came home and found me on the upper balcony. "Maggie, I want you to come back inside because I have something exciting to tell you."

"Well, tell me right here"

"No, I want to make sure you don't jump off the balcony."

"Oh, no, you are going back to Idaho?"

"No, we are moving to Colorado!

Close your mouth, you'll catch a fly"

"Why?"

I'm tired of Arkansas politics, and I have been offered several judgeships in Colorado."

I just sat down on the nearest chair and looked at him. "Exactly where is Colorado? Is it up by Idaho?" I said sarcastically.

"No, sweetheart, it is on the other side of Kansas and you know where Kansas is. We'll even go through there on our way, and you can meet some of my old friends."

I decided I wasn't going to scream and fuss like I did when Tom announced we were moving to Idaho. Thank goodness I never had to go there.

"How soon are we leaving?"

Tom seemed relieved. "I think we can leave in two weeks or so."

"What about this wonderful house?"

"What do you want to do with it?"

"I hope we keep it because we might not like Colorado, so we'll have something to come back to."

"Maggie, let's sell this house and I promise to build you a mansion in Colorado."

Tom went on to say that he could prove to me that trains did indeed have dining cars. He had told me they did when we were fighting about his going to Idaho and I did not believe him. Tom had told me once that he never lied to me about anything, but he didn't always tell me everything there was to know about something. To my complete surprise there were dining cars on the trains. A more modern world seemed to be descending upon the nation.

CHAPTER 11

BEAUTIFUL COLORADO

I loved Colorado the minute I stepped off the train. The air was so crisp and clear. I had never seen mountains that high or so awe striking. It was a whole new beginning and one that I was eager to start. Tom became the Judge of the Fourth Judicial District which was great, except Tom had to travel a lot. The towns where courts were held were so far apart. He always had a translator with him as he didn't speak Spanish, the language of the territory. We both set a goal of learning to speak Spanish as soon as possible.

Tom wanted to wait and build a house later when he knew more about the town and the region. He promised we would not go back to Arkansas. One thing I would not miss was the humidity. In Arkansas, you could take a bath, get out of the tub, dry yourself completely off, but five minutes later you were dripping with water again. I had to get use the snow; I had seen snow before but never in that quantity or depth.

We moved into a boarding house which I considered a step below me, but, at least, I didn't have to cook or clean. Being surrounded by so many people, and the walls so thin, meant we had to be quiet when making love. We weren't use to that. At least we wouldn't be living there forever. Since he had to travel the judicial circuit it was best I not be stuck some place alone.

There was a lovely young widow living at the boarding house, too. Her name was Josephine Payne. Her husband, Lewis, had been killed while prospecting for gold. He apparently lost his balance and fell off a cliff. She was quite open about the fact that she was looking for a new husband. Several Mormon men approached her about becoming one of their wives, but she would have no part of that.

Josephine vowed she would never go back to her home state of Virginia because of the strict social code. Her family had only been there for two generations, so they were looked down upon. She and I formed a friendship. There wasn't much to do in Denver for proper ladies. We spent most of our time irritating the clerks in what stores they had. Single men, Anglos, were the first settlers of Colorado. They had come mainly to make it rich in mining, or to get way from whatever was chasing them back home. Women as wives came later, only after the men got tired of the whores, who were in plentiful supply. However, those women wouldn't wash their socks or cook their meals, so they had to take wives.

Josephine was so pretty it didn't take long for her to find a man to her liking. One night at the supper table, we were joined by Charles Billingsley who was in town to hire some more men for his mine at Cripple Creek. Josephine caught his eye, he proposed, and she said yes. He wasn't as handsome as Tom, but fairly good looking. It turned out he was a cousin to Mrs. Young who ran the boarding house. She vouched for his character.

Tom and I stood up with them when they got married at the courthouse. They stayed in her room at the boarding house on their wedding night. It was obvious at breakfast the next morning that things had gone well, because they were both beaming. After breakfast they left for Cripple Creek. We saw them again a number of years later at a miners' convention. By then they had four children and Tom had become famous as a miner and very wealthy, although none of us could have imagined any of that as they drove off.

Although Tom had savings, the pay as a judge wasn't very much. He supplemented our income by playing a lot of poker. He usually had to play with some of the new men moving into Denver, because most of men in town refused to play with him again. They knew they would lose money.

One night an old man, whose front teeth were missing, was so desperate to win, and so sure of his hand, put the deed to his undeveloped mine into the betting pool. Tom won, as usual, and the old man threw up his hands and said, "Sonny, you just got took. That deed is valid, but there ain't no gold in that region. I've been searching for gold there for nearly a year. It just ain't there."

Tom didn't think much about it, but put it into his legal pouch to look at it while on his trip to Pueblo the next day. He took the deed out and realized the old man's mistake. He was probably illiterate, and didn't understand latitude and longitude and had the directions backwards. Tom realized the deed was for land just north of Pueblo. Whether there was gold there was another matter.

Tom located the area but didn't know very much about mining so he hired Ross Hardin, an assayer. The next morning Ross met Tom at the front of the Court House and asked to speak to him privately. The man glanced around to make sure there was no one in earshot who spoke English.

"Judge Harwell, the area is loaded with gold. I dug down about ten feet and struck a vein of pure gold."

Tom thought the man was either a liar or a charlatan. Then Ross pulled several chucks of gold from his pocket for proof. Tom said he was just dumfounded. After court finished, Tom and Ross went down the hall and registered the deed, and formed a partnership. They kept the find as quiet as possible, but Tom took the precaution of hiring a guard to keep everyone out of the mine area.

Tom tried to find the old man that he won the deed from but he seemed to have disappeared. The deed had been made out to a John Smith, which more than likely was not his real name. Tom searched the Denver area and finally found some men that the toothless man had been camping with on Cherry Creek. They didn't know his name. People weren't quick to give their names to strangers. One of the men said the old man had joined up with a wagon train headed west. Tom was puzzled as to where west would be, because going through the Colorado Mountains wasn't easily done. West could mean anywhere, so Tom gave up looking.

For a time, we continued to live in the boarding house so as not to arouse suspicion. Then, Tom gave up his judgeship and we moved to Pueblo so he could concentrate his energies on building the Annie Jacobs Mine.

"Why did you pick that name?" I asked

"It's after the steamboat that I saved when we came under attack by the Rebels on the Arkansas River. We lost the other two."

Tom thought that the name Annie Jacobs would bring him luck. As it turned out, he had already had his luck. The more Tom and Ross looked for gold, the more they found. The newspaper said it was one of the Wonders of the World and said the mine was worth twenty million dollars. I thought that was about one of the dumbest things in the world.

Tom asked me why I would think such a thing.

"Because there is no such thing as twenty million dollars anywhere on earth." I stated.

Tom just laughed at me and asked if I would like to go buy some furniture. I flipped around and left the room. After all these years, he just had to bring that up!

He built me a mansion just like he said he would. The mining operation got so big Tom had to keep hiring men. The miners were required to empty their pockets every night to keep them from stealing a lot of gold. Tom figured they were sneaking out small pieces anyway. The assayer officers in the area were on alert if a miner started showing up with too much gold at one time.

One night Tom came home and said, "There's a black man at the mine who says he knows you"

"Knows me? How on earth?" I replied.

'He said his name was Samuel Freeman, and he knew you back in Van Buren." said Tom.

"There wasn't a colored family in Van Buren named Freeman."

"He said his parents were slaves of your family."

"Oh, My God! That's Aunt Marie and Uncle Henry's boy! I wonder if they know where he is." I exclaimed. "Of course I know Samuel, we grew up together so to speak."

"He said he would like to see you."

"Of course, but it would never do to have him come to the house. Is there someplace else we could meet? I don't think a woman should go to the mine."

"A true Southern girl to the end!" laughed Tom.

"There are a number of woman who hang around the mine, but they aren't ladies." Said chuckled

"That's awful. Can't you run them off?"

"Sweetheart, do we have to have that discussion again? I will leave well enough alone." Tom said emphatically. "I need happy workers."

"I'll find a place where you and Sam can talk. He is one of the best workers I have. He is already singled out for promotion."

"That's because he was raised right! His parents didn't put up with any nonsense"

———◇———

Tom and Ross already had a bookkeeper, but Tom decided they needed a real accountant to oversee all the money transactions. I always thought Ross looked pale and unhealthy so I wasn't surprised when he was diagnosed with consumption. However, I was surprised that he went so quickly. He had never married and said he was an orphan, so whatever Tom wanted to do with his share of the money he could. After Ross died, Tom built a large park in downtown Denver and named it the Ross Hardin Park. It is a lovely place.

One morning Tom told me he had hired a young man, who had graduated from Notre Dame, to be an accountant for the mining company. The man was to arrive the next day. Later the same day, there was a knock at the door, and when I opened it I thought I was seeing an apparition. There stood a tall, handsome man with a head full of curly black hair. The apparition spoke and said, "Mrs. Harwell, my name is Harris McGinity." I promptly fainted. Harris called for help. Tom and Mildred, our house-keeper came running. Tom was sure I had died; Harris lifted me up and placed me on the chaise in the sun room. Mildred brought me a glass of water. Tom took one look at Harris and realized why I had fainted. Harris looked just like his father, John, who had been Tom's best friend and a Major in his unit during the war. We had introduced Carolyn Harris to John McGinty while the 13th Kansas was stationed a Van Buren, Arkansas. Tom and I had felt guilty for his suicide. Carolyn had gone across the river to her great grandmother's home at Barling, Arkansas. We had received word that she delivered prematurely and the baby had died. That baby now stood in the middle of our sun room. How it happened that Harris knew where we lived came to light much later.

I asked Harris where he was staying. "Tom said for me to check into the Denver Hotel, so I did."

I closed my eyes when it dawned on me that Tom had known about Harris all along. I was delighted that John's baby had lived and deeply angry that Tom hadn't told me. He knew how much I had grieved over John's and the baby's death.

When I closed my eyes everyone thought I had fainted again. It's a wonder I hadn't. I was just as shocked.

Tom stood slightly out of every one's eyesight and shook his head slightly to signal that I shouldn't say anything about knowing his unmarried parents or about his father's suicide and his mother's treachery.

The next day, Tom converted the sun room into an office and that was where Harris worked as the chief accountant for Bowen Mining Company.

There was not any way I could have foreseen the strange twist and turns our lives would take. The baby that didn't die totally changed our lives and changed Harris' life too.

Thank you for reading Mary Margaret Book Two.
Please take a moment and leave your review of the book on <u>Amazon</u>.

Other books in the Mary Margaret series:
Miss Mary Margaret Marries A Yankee—available on Amazon
Book Three is scheduled to be released in 2014.

You can stay up-to-date on release information by connecting with
Mary Frances Hodges through:
<u>Facebook</u> Mary Frances Hodges, Author
<u>Twitter</u> @MaryFHodges
<u>Google+</u> Mary Frances Hodges
And through her website <u>http://maryfranceshodges.com</u>